Title.

The Cheeks Heat

By Zeeshan Ali

One

The motion of chairs scrapping against the ground makes me soar. I rub my eyes only to realise I'm in my math elegance. My eyes widen for a 2d and go searching. People are leaving the class and some are giving me bizarre stares. My cheeks heat up and I quickly take hold of my books which are scattered on my table.

"Ms. Evans?" A voice says from the the front of the room. I look up to look my math trainer, Ms. Grace, giving me a loss of life glare. I bow my head slightly and stroll as much as her.

"Yes?" I squeak.

"I'm going to should provide you with detention for napping in my class." She says writing on a chunk of paper. I do not say some thing as she palms me the slip of paper and she turns returned to her paintings. I make a dash for the door however do not make it some distance out once I come upon someone.

"Sorry." I mumble beneath my breath and try to circulate out of the way.

"Hey! Watch where you are going!" A high pitched voice says. I turn my interest to the shining, yellow headed, famous woman of our college.

Hazel Copper. She has vivid yellow hair and eyes the color of ice. She become the epitome of your standard stereotype girl. She wears the maximum obnoxious garments and these days she is sporting a purple brief sleeved crop top and a infant blue skirt. She looks like cotton candy. I might by no means want to be her. Ever.

"Sorry." I mumble again and try to flow away from her and her minions.

"Hey, don't go Madilyn." She says to me.

"Yeah. Don't cross." Bell Grenn says from at the back of Hazel. Her dark brown eyes have an evil smirk hidden in them. She has wild curly hair slicked lower back right into a tight bun and her coffee colored skin is wrapped in tight washed blue jeans and a shiny pink shoulder strapless top.

"Sorry however I must. I need to get to my subsequent class." I say to them with my head nonetheless down.

"Fine. Suit your self and get your brains washed with vain information." Kellen Corst says from in the back of Hazel. She has light brown hair dyed blue on the guidelines. Her amber eyes are the nicest out of the three, however her garments are not any better. She has on black shorts with a mustard yellow tank top. I roll my eyes at the trio. I push beyond them and at the remaining minute I trap them rolling their eyes in sink at me. I quick and quietly make my manner to my 2nd magnificence.

•*•*•

I was capable of live awake at some stage in history which turned into superb boring. All we did changed into pay attention to the instructor examine monotonously. I nearly fell asleep twice. I now make my manner down the corridor to my 1/3 elegance of the day.

Finally! Next is lunch! I silently cheer in my head. I make it to my class a few minutes early. I take a seat inside the returned and take out my e-book. I pay attention a commotion going on out of doors and shortly input Hazel, Bell and Kellen. They look over at me and provide a faux smile. I mentally bash my head at the table as I provide them a small smile returned. They walk over to me and sit down down in desks round me.

"So. How become washing your brain?" Kellen asks at the same time as looking to stifle a laugh.

"Good. Very informative." I say giving a fake smile and using as an awful lot of enthusiasm in my voice. Bell and Hazel roll their eyes as Kellen turns far from us to speak to some other women throughout from her.

"You ought to get a few buddies." Hazel informs me and Bell laughs.

"Thanks." I say and turning to the board. Mr. Berg walks in and we begin the lesson. My eyelids sense heavy and soon I am awoken by way of the bell ringing. I leap by using the bell and a bit bit of water goes flying out of my fingers onto the ground. I appearance far from it and disguise my palms. I hear Hazel guffawing as she walks out of the door with her minions. I roll my eyes and begin to depart myself while Mr. Berg calls me.

"Yes?" I ask nervously.

"Are you adequate?" He asks. "Because you slept thru my class and I heard from your math trainer that you slept via her class and she or he gave you detention. And then your history instructor stuck you dozing some times." He explains my morning.

"Yes I'm excellent. I simply failed to get enough sleep." I lie partially. I did not sleep in any respect remaining night. A cold sit back kept going up my lower back and I felt a presence inside or outside my room. Instead of going to sleep, I practiced controlling my water.

"Ok. I didn't need to provide you greater detention." He says. "Oh, and also Mr. Grubbs has requested I inform you to move see him after lunch." My eyes widen at this and he need to've visible it.

"You are not in hassle Ms. Evans. He best wants to see you after lunch. Your chemistry instructor is aware of you'll be a little overdue for her magnificence." I let loose a breath I failed to recognise I became protecting.

"Thank you." I say.

"Your welcome Madilyn." He smiles kindly and I walk out of his class to lunch nonetheless wondering what Mr. Grubbs wants with me. I wasn't looking where I changed into going and some thing journeys me. I fall at the ground with a hard thud.

Ouch. I assume to myself as I select myself up ignoring the laughs coming from human beings in the back of me as I make my way to the cafeteria.

TWO

"Mr. Grubbs?" I ask after knocking.

"Come in," says his everyday scratchy voice.

I open the door and notice he's doing paper work at his very cluttered table. I take a seat down in considered one of his two comfy chairs across from him. His office is littered in papers. Some are mendacity loosely on his desks and some are on his shelves behind his table.

Mr. Grubbs is an older man and in his 50's. He does not have an awful lot hair left on his head. Only a few stubble and along his chin to form a genuinely hideous beard. Mr. Grubbs is the sort of primary that constantly wants pleasant for the scholars at RiverCliff Junior High School.

"You asked to look me?" I say reminding him while he seems up from his paper work searching at me, confusion evident on his face.

I forgot to say. He has a touch bit of brief time period memory misplaced. It isn't always critical however it does get a bit bad occasionally. He generally has to put in writing stuff down and I have no concept how he does it cluttered with many papers.

"Ohhh.... Sure Madilyn. Right, right, proper. One second Ms. Evans." He tells me getting up from his seat to get greater papers from his dark all rightshelves and talking to himself, while waving a finger, "Here. Ok. First of we're going to have a foreign exchange pupil coming to our college. I idea that since you are a virtually correct scholar, instantly A's, by no means missing some thing, no longer lacking a single day of faculty, that you can excursion him around." He tells me, "Oh and he can be in all your lessons so you can show him the whole lot and be his buddy. How does that sound?"

I take a look at him with my jaw actually on the ground.

What????? Why me? Why not Hazel or absolutely everyone else, however me!!! I assume to myself.

"Ummm....." I start, "What is his name?" I ask before saying yes.

"Jayden MaZinn." He tells me.

He sounds like that supper cute, terrible boy on the way to cross after Hazel. Urgh!!! I suppose.

"How long will he be here?"

"His own family is moving from Australia. And he goes to be right here for the relaxation of the yr."

Oh remarkable an accessory! And he is staying! Great! Just what my life desires! I bitch to myself.

"Fine, I'll do it." I tell Mr. Grubbs. And the handiest motive I am doing it's so once he gets buddies and all the girls pass after him, a good way to be the first day of school, he'll depart me on my own and by no means ever ought to intervene in my life ever again.

"Ok. It's settled then." Mr Grubbs says. I provide him a decent smile and arise from my seat to mention thank you to him before strolling out the door to chemistry with a frown taking up my face.

.*.*.

I couldn't take the bus home because I had detention. It changed into terrible. I needed to catch up on the whole thing that I neglected at some stage in the day because I saved sound asleep off in the course of each magnificence despite meals in me. I am now on foot down a street of Tofino. The sky is a dark grey and is spitting out tiny droplets of rain. It appears to be mocking me as the rain get heavier. Instead of focusing at the rain and the terrible day I had, I decide to assume.

I start to think about this Jayden. Wondering what he looks as if and the way he will act around me, the non-social female.

I hope he doesn't note my palms. I suppose, searching at my fingers. Nothing is wrong with them at the outside but it's the inner. I can control water. I do not know how or why I simply can. I have not instructed each person about it due to the fact when I attempted to inform my first-rate friend in Grade School, she left me.

I was too busy wondering that when I became the nook I failed to realize that I bumped into a person till I hit the slick pavement.

"You adequate?" A closely accented voice asked. "I did not see you there."

I open my eyes to peer brown
eyes observing me.

"Yes." I tell them.

A hand is prolonged out to me and I grab it, grateful for the help. I
look up and this boy around my age, 14-15, appears lower back at
me with the ones brown eyes. For a few cause the eyes look faux
and I do not know why. He has red-brown hair that falls onto his
face. He additionally has this perfect smile so that it will make
women go ballistic over. He has on a jean jacket covering a simple
white t-blouse with a few jeans at the side of black speak that look
new and smooth as compared to my grimy blue ones. He looks
like the suitable model.

"What's your name?" His accented voice asks.

Oh!!! Wow his accessory is so crisp and sharp!!!

I kept looking at this stunning famous person stranger, till I found
out I need to appear to be a freak. I fast regarded into those faux
eyes.

What is inaccurate with his eyes?

"Umm...Howdy? Are you good enough?" The stranger says
waving a hand in my face.

"Oh....!!!! Sorry! I-I changed into wondering. S-sorry about th-that." I stutter looking lower back at him. His hair is falling on pinnacle of his head because of the rain falling closely now.

"Oh it's adequate." He says guffawing it off, "Soooo....What is your call?" He asked again.

I did not want to inform this stranger my name.

I determine to tell him the primary call that came to my head. And that took place to be my mothers, "Poppy Evans." I say.

"Hmm..." he says, "You do not appear to be a Poppy. Not to be rude but with your black hair, darkish freckles, and water blue eyes.....You do not look like one." He says narrowing his eyes and going a bit quiet as he says water blue eyes. No one has ever defined my eyes like that.

"Well, thanks." I say no longer being indignant due to the fact my name is not Poppy.

He looks at me suspiciously and I begin to get uncomfortable while he maintains gazing me.

"Well.....Exceptional to meet you." I say to him, shifting around him to get domestic.

I preserve feeling his eyes on me until I turn the corner to my avenue.

I keep strolling down the sidewalk when I sense a chilly sit back move down my spin.

I turn round to see if all and sundry was there and no one was. I get scared and start on foot down quicker, turning my head every five seconds.

I am half of way to my house when I pay attention footsteps in the back of me. I turn around again, panicking and see nobody is there. I stay there shocked.

What the heck!!! I assume. What's occurring? Am I being followed?

I flip around and run the relaxation of the distance to my residence, terrified. And the complete manner I hear a person following, but every time I flip my head around it is simply me on the road.

I eventually attain my house and slam the door shut.

"Madi?" My father's calm voice asks.

Three

"Madi?" My father's calm voice calls.

I am breathing difficult and can not pay attention him. I just take a seat with my again to the door, panting with my eyes huge open.

"Madi?" My father calls from the kitchen.

Wait why is my dad home early? He is never home early? What goes on? I recognize.

"Madi?!?" My father says panicking and walking to me. He reveals me on the door and hugs me tight.

"Madi? What goes on?" My father asked involved.

I come to my senses and talk to him, "Nothing I simply thought I heard some thing outside and I were given scared and ran all the way home."

"Why did not you get at the bus?" He asked harassed pulling away.

"I wanted to consider a few matters and the bus is to loud every so often." I say to him searching into his hazel-blue eyes.

"Well simply get at the bus from now on, good enough?" He asks.

"Fiiiiiiine" I groan. "And why are you here early? You are by no
means right here early."

"Oh..Sure...I....Uh..G-were given the day of today. And so I
determined to have some dad time and wager what?" He says,
stuttering a little.

I stare at him stupidly and say, "what?"

"I'm making dinner!!!" He says incredible exited with jazz fingers.
He even gets up and starts to bounce.

My dad is a funny guy. He wants all people to snicker. He's
outgoing and talks to almost all and sundry. He is the alternative of
me. He has hazel-blue eyes, brown hair and a moustache. He hates
it although, so he usually shaves.

"Urggggggggh!!!" I say, trying to be funny.

"Hey!!!! I am indignant!!!!" He says, turning his back to me,
crossing his fingers and setting his chin up within the air.
"Humph."

We can not ever stay extreme for long, so in one 2d we are on the
ground rolling round laughing with tears in our eyes.

"Oh, Madi!" He says hugging me, "I love you so much!"

"I love you to daddy!" I say to him, hugging him returned.

We stay hugging for a little bit due to the fact we never get this time. He is always home late and leaves within the morning early.

"I'm domestic, Madi!" My mother's voice comes from the storage location.

My dad gets up and places his finger to his lips signalling to maintain stop due to the fact he is home. Even mom in no way sees him.

"Hi mom, I simply got home." I yell, on foot to the returned to locate her.

"Oh honey, I love you!" She says hugging me, "What do you need for dinner dad is not ho-what is that odor?" She asked interrupting herself, strolling to the kitchen.

She starts offevolved to move within the kitchen doorway whilst my dad jumps out from the entrance. To be sincere I actually have in no way heard my mom scream that loud. The scream can be wrong for a robber breaking into our house.

"Jesus, Deven!!!" My mom yells, "what the heck!!!"

"Surprise!!!!" My dad says again with jazz hands.

My family loves making jokes. My dad holds my mother in a huge embody.

My mother has blonde hair that is died brown on the tips making it aumbry. She has thick glasses that cover her blue eyes. Just like mine.

I do not know why I actually have black hair, each my dad and mom do not have black hair and most of my other own family is blonde, and blue eyes. Well as that guy in the road said, water blue eyes, and I actually have started out to word it approximately my mom's too. People have always stated we have similar eyes, but by no means have I idea because it as water.

"Madi, are available in her you girly!" My dad says to me.

I walk over to them and that they embody me and I embrace them.

"So what's for dinner?" My mom asked liberating from our hug. "To be sincere it smells genuinely right."

"Spaghetti!" My father says look very proud.

"Oh exact! At least that may be a step up from the only other component you could make, mac n' cheese." She says ironically, walking over to the range and looking into the pot.

"Wow, Pop!" My dad says, "I can not agree with you!!"

We all burst out into giggling, once more.

.*.*.

I sit in my room observing my ceiling. It's a little slanted but I love it. I actually have painted a galaxy with planets and stars on after I became eleven. My dad of route had to assist me with it. I adore it so much.

Dinner become superb. We stored giggling and joking around. We ended up throwing spaghetti at my dad for fun.

"Hey pricey," my mom says entering my room, "Are you accomplished with your homework?"

"Oh ya, I am." I inform her.

"Ok, right. I am going out now, so I wanted to make sure you have been done."

"Oh ya and I might not live up studying overdue I promise! I love you mom!"

"I love you too!" She says closing the door behind her.

I quick begin to get geared up for mattress doing my regular routine and getting my e-book.

I examine for about 20-30 minutes once I get this cold sit back once more like remaining night time. But as soon as it is there it's far long past.

I cross appearance out my window and see that the boy I ran into turned into passing my residence. He looks up to me and smiles. I quick duck down and move slowly to my mattress.

Who is he? And how does he know in which I stay? What's taking place? I preserve questioning myself.

I move over to my mattress and sit down. I start grabbing moister from the air and forming it right into a pug. I have constantly wanted one but my dad and mom have in no way let me have one. I make sure to get the specified of the face perfect. I then try and put as lots attention into it and then the pug is cuddling in my lap.

"Yes!" I say excitedly. I have made the water animate and live in shape without dripping water. Of direction it will disappear and not using a awareness. I lay in my bed ready for sleep to wash over me. The pug cuddles in my palms, the slick water just barely touching my arm. I slowly fall into unconsciousness, very privy to the water canine slowly dripping water onto my mattress.

.*.*.

"Hello Mr. Grubbs." I say walking inside the the front door he asked me to go into to meet Jayden.

I woke up this mourning to a large puddles of water beside me. I needed to slowly pull it out of my sheet and put it again in the air.

"Oh hey Ms. Evans, how are you these days?" Mr. Grubbs asks with courtesy.

"Good."

"Ok properly Jayden said he became going for walks a bit late so why don't you pass right down to your locker and I'll call for you when he comes."

"Oh, ok." I say beginning to stroll down the corridor to my magnificence.

I simply get to my locker to put my things away when Hazel has to come across me making me spill the whole thing I changed into keeping.

"Oops! Sorry bout that! I'll can help you smooth that up!" She says placing a hand to her too pink lips.

Wow!

I start to smooth up my matters when any other hand starts offevolved to choose them as much as. I appearance up to be met with a pair of fake brown eyes.

Huh!!! Who is tha-

It all happened so speedy, I stumble back and my palms arise for reflexes and water goes flying out of my arms. It turns to ice, as I pay attention, and hits the boy at his brow.

Everyone begins to stare at me and I live there frozen. Then I make a dash to the women toilet and lock the stall door.

Oh nononononono!!!!! How can I let myself try this in front of anyone!!!!! And how did I make it ice? I've never accomplished that before?

After about 5 mins I hear a voice, "Ummm.... Madilyn are you in here?" Says a crisp accented voice.

How????

"Come on. I realize you're in that stall Madilyn."

I live first rate silent attempting now not to make a valid.

Someone begins banging on my stall door.

"Come on out Madilyn!" Says the accented voice angrily

I quick open the door to be met with the ones fake brown eyes once more.

"Ahhh you have to be Madilyn Evans?" He asks. "I am Jayden MaZinn as you realize."

"How do you recognize my name?" I ask quietly and curious.

"Ha! I understand plenty greater about you and your mother than you understand. And also I understand your name isn't Poppy." He says to me.

"S-Sorry. Poppy is my mom's call." I inform him.

"Wait your mom?" He asks harassed, "Her call is Poppy?"

"Ya Poppy Evans. And how do you know her?"

"Oh....Ummm......K."He says dragging out the a, "Like I stated I understand greater approximately you than you realize!"

"That doesn't make any feel!" I yell.

"Madilyn. Calm down. Ok. Now I need you to include me right now." He says sternly looking at me with an excessive glare.

"Why?" I ask backing away into the stall.

"Because. Now come!" He says getting indignant once more.

And he's telling me to relax! Wow!

"Nooo!!!" I yell, pushing at his chest, "Get away!!!"

"Will you come if I had been to tell you there are others such as you?" He asks.

"What?"

Four

"What?" I say once more.

"Come." He says with a grin on his face.

I'm to bowled over to move, however come what may my legs pass for me and I am staring blankly at not anything.

21

"Ok we're going to have to undergo the window so no person can see us. That already knows approximately your water." He says to me.

I stop in my tracks making
him stumble a bit. "Are you want me?" I ask apparently, not registering something he simply stated to me.

"Huh. Ahhh......I changed into kinda afraid you will ask that. But.....Ya. A little."

"What do you suggest? Can you now not do this?" I say grabbing some moister from the air and forming a ball and throwing it at his forehead again.

"OWWWW!!!!" He says rubbing his brow.

"Oops! Sorry! Didn't mean to do that!" I say satirically.

"Where did you study that?" He asks curiously.

"Eh, discovered it myself."

"Okay. Well I am kinda the same as you, however now not the equal Element." He tells me. He begins to transport his fingers back and forth around my face and soon sufficient infront of my eyes he is keeping a ball of fire.

"Hey! Now don't throw that!" I yelped, stepping again.

"Hahahahah!!!! Oh my god!! To humorous!! Us Fire Elementals don't throw our hearth at other Elementals.

"Elementals?" I ask tilting my head.

"Enough questions. Someone will answer that once we get to Externilia." He says pushing me in the direction of the window. "Now we are going to believe ourselves end up engulf into the Light and let the Wind take our particles away.

The Light Elementals have talked to the sun, yes earlier than you may ask the Light Elementals speak Light and the Wind communicate Wind, the Earth talk Earth , the Water speak Water, the Fire communicate Fire, and the Darkness communicate Darkness. We have like a second language built into us. Anyway.....The Lights have talked to the Sun and asked if they might spoil down Elementals debris after which the Winds have talked to the Wind and Air to hold us to Elementa." He explains to me.

"What's Elementa and Externilia?" I say teasing him.

"Wow. Come on. Now just ensure to tell the Light to absorb your body and tell the Wind in which you need to head. You have to speak absolutely so the Wind and Light can apprehend you due to the fact you and I aren't Winds or Lights."

"Ok. Wait in which do we pass?" I ask a bit apprehensive.

24

"Say Externilia, Elementa."

I stand within the mild felling the nice and cozy air take in my frame. I stand for what looks like 5 mins and then after I feel the Wind coming and washing over my body I inform both of them to bring me to Externilia, Elementa. I cross fast and quietly out the window and it looks like nothing and I am remarkable secure. Until I start to loose fall downwards I try to scream. But I can not seam to get the air into my lungs and I begin to panic. I try to flail round but my frame components do not flow. Then for some motive I am calmed by way of the Wind and the Sun. I sense mild and sense like I can fly. It feels superb to be particles.

"Wow" I says out loud. My voice sounds clear and I do not have to grasp for air anymore.

"We understand" says a light flowy voice.

All of a sudden I am placed at the floor lightly by way of the Wind and Light. I sense my body coming returned collectively and I have so much electricity I feel like I can run marathon.

It's bizarre.

I turn round to peer the Wind and Light. They appear like tiny particles floating out of thin air. The Wind is a mild gray and the Light is a pale yellow. They don't have any face, they just seem like floating debris against the lushes inexperienced grass.

I let loose a gasp and stumble returned. They quick rush to choose me back up onto my ft.

"Thank you?" I query. They nod and disappear into nothingness.

"What simply befell?" I says out loud. I am confused for a few minutes when I recognise I am status in front of a glittering fort standing on a lushes green hill with a stone route main as much as it.

The castle is top notch tall. It blocks the solar from my eyes. But rather it glitters from the sun. It seems to have all sorts of matters in it, water, fire, light, nature, wind, and darkness. It all seems embedded into the crystals and gemstones.

"Woah!!" I say breathless looking round. I quickly recognize Jayden is not right here.

"Jayden!" I yell for him.

"Here!" Comes a voice out of thin air. And literally Jayden pops out of thin air touchdown on his bum.

"Owww!!!" He cries out. "Wow the Wind and Light can be so suggest to us other Elementals. Oh and how will you speak Wind and light?" He questions.

"I just said Externilia, Elementa as you stated to do."I inform him imparting a hand.

He takes it and says, "Huh. Ok then. Come with me I am now going to show you the citadel and the castle village, the cites surrounding the citadel village and our natural habitats." He says main me to the castles massive the front spruce doorways.

.*.*.

We walk through the huge double spruce doorways, and already someone jumps on Jayden.

They begin to roll at the ground and fight a little until Jayden pins the man or woman down and starts offevolved tickling him,

"Ahhh...Jay!!!....Come....On....I...I'm sorry....Ahhhhhhh!!!!!!......JAY!!!!" The character yells between suits of laughter.

Jayden receives off of him and stands out a hand to assist him up.

"Yo, Jay, what's up along with your eyes." The man or woman says looking closely into Jayden's eyes.

"Oh ya I forgot." He says putting his finger to 1 eye. I have to appearance away because I cannot stand people touching there eyes.

"Done." I flip around to be met with blasting orange eyes. I stumble lower back and that is while the brand new man or woman notices me.

That's why they looked fake. He turned into sporting contacts that protected his real eyes

"And who may this be?" He asks stepping nearer best for me to step again.

"This is Madilyn Evans and-hiya!!! A, no. She's only just came and look at her hair and eyes." He tells this A man or woman.

"Hey, sorry I'm Aaron Cross-Lang." He says placing a hand out so I can shake it. I do not shake it.

"Sorry bout that." He says pulling his hand lower back in embarrassment. He places his hand into a pocket that looks like it's miles just barely conserving on.

Aaron has muddy brown hair that sticks up in spiky clumps and hazel-inexperienced eyes. He has on a operating device belt and along side some overalls that go over a actually ugly yellow t-shirt.

His boots are included and crusted with mud. He is about the hight as Jayden however only a little bit smaller. Still he's taller than me.

"Aaron is a Earth Element." Jayden says to me noticing my curiosity,

"Wait!!!" Aaron says alarmed, "You have black hair and water blue eyes!!!"

"Aaron!!! Stop that!" Jayden says even as punching him within the arm.

"Well you kinda cannot omit in. She has blue eyes, meaning one in every of her parents are Water. And she has BLACK hair, which means that the opposite one is Darkness." Aaron explains to Jayden who looks like he already is aware of approximately this.

"Well...Ummmm.....I actually have a dad names Deven Evans, and a mom named Poppy Evans but they both do not know I can manipulate water." I say shyly.

They both stare at me like I'm loopy.

"Come Madilyn, Aaron get again to work and I'm going to take Madilyn to Queen Bee." Jayden says pulling me with him.

"Really. Now your telling me to paintings. I have already got half of the fort saying that to me." He shouts back at us, "I thought we wherein buddies!" He playfully states.

"Ignore him." Jayden says to me.

I burst out giggling at them and Jayden simply appears at me weirdly.

"H-how.....C......An.............Y-y-you sta-y......Critical...For s-o-o-o lo-o-o-ong!!!!!" I strive to talk between laughters. I emerge as falling over because I'm laughing to plenty and 2 fingers trap me earlier than I can contact the floor.

"What?" Jayden asks confused seeking to placed me on my feet whilst I hold giggling out loud.

"Oh you wo-ouldn't recognize. My family is all jokes. We usually try to make each different giggle due to the fact it is also my mother and I domestic and my dad is careworn all of the time. So every time we can get the risk we crack jokes." I provide an explanation for to him, wiping the tears from my eyes that I have not noticed have shape. I become thinking to much and my feelings can normally get the first-class of me and after I think of something definitely sensitive, I tear up.

"Hey. Madilyn, your here. It's where you belong." Jayden tells me, wrapping his fingers around me.

"Ya. I realize, however what approximately dad and mom?" I query.

"Oh well......We will speak to Queen Bee approximately that." He tells me.

"Who's that?"

"Like I said. Questions later. We want to get to her. We have a meeting set up to satisfy her today and we do not need to be past due." He tells me beginning to tug me down a long alway.

We skip huge alrightdoors before everything with paintings at the walls. We then turn left and find our selves facing a grand dinning hall.

"Wrong way. Sorry even I get mixed up from time to time." Jayden says spinning me round to go proper.

We then are met with a grand stair case that results in so many hallways and doors. We maintain on foot up those stairs until we reach the remaining hallway on the pinnacle.

"Down this hallway is the Royal circle of relatives corridors. Lots of Elementals stay within the castle and that is reserved for the real Royal family. Oh and Art Ella is the Queens son. He is my age and snobby. He thinks he's higher than all of us due to the fact he is the Queens son. So just ignore him." Jayden tells me transferring to the remaining door. "Oh and don't call the Queen, Queen Beemia. She loathes being known as Beemia. So just call her Queen Bee."

He goes to knock on the door while he is interrupted with the aid of a sudden voice coming from behind us.

"Well isn't it Jayden MaZinn."

We both turn round to be met by a man around Jayden's age. He has pale yellow hair and light yellow eyes. He has this lovely smirk that indicates of his brilliant lovable dimples. He is about Jaydens hight and wonderful handsome.

"Well, good day Art. We are simply going to head see your mother, so if we ought to now go and we can speak to you later!" Jayden says absolutely weirdly. He then starts to show me around prepared to knock on the door once more.

"Wait, Wait, Wait. Who is this lovable girl proper right here." Art says to Jayden. He then attempts to show me round and does efficiently and looks into my eyes. He the smirks, "Well, well, properly. Who can we have here?" He questions.

I do not even attempt to solution and thank god Jayden stepped in.

"This is Madilyn Evans. She is new to this international so if you can please let us cross see your mom." Jayden tells Art.

"Oh. Ok, properly I'll goodbye." He says to us moving towards any other door on the left and is going into what I expect is his room.

"Urgh. I hate him." Jayden grumps.

"Why?" I ask curiously.

"I'll tell you later. Now Queen Bee is awaiting us." He says knocking at the big dark okaywood door in the front of us.

"Come in!!" Says a excessive pitched voice.

Jayden pushes open the darkish okaydoors quite simply that look like they manner a thousand pounds.

"Hello Queen Bee, lovable to look you once more." Jayden says politely to the Queen with a bow. But she is not looking at him, she is asking at me with curiosity in her eyes.

And worry.

Five

"Uhhhhhh......" I say awkwardly, trying to break the silence between us. The Queen is like frozen in her place staring at me with so much worry and curiosity plastered on her face, "Sooooo......."

"Oh....umm....sorry about that dear. You must see my emotions plastered all over my face like I see on yours. Wait what Element are you?" Her high pitched voice asks.

"Uhh......Water." I say.

"Then how can I see your emotions like playing all over your face. Us Lights are really bad at keeping our emotions under control and Waters are very good. You must've a mixture of Light and Water. But how do you have black hair and water blue eyes?" She questions.

"I don't know." I say, "I just got here."

"Sorry," She says staring intently at my face."It's just that you look so much like him."

She has on this elegant gown that looks like it is made of sunlight that reaches her ankles showing of her bare feet. Her yellow flowing hair reaches down to her bum and is in nice gentle waves. She has thin glasses that cover glowing yellow eyes.

"Uh, ok...ummm.....Queen Bee? Are you ok?" Jayden asks.

"Oh yes dear. Umm can you let Madilyn and I have this time together. You can just wait outside or go visit Art. He should be in his room." Queen Bee says waving Jayden of with her hand.

"Okaaaaaay......." Jayden says leaving. He starts to shut the door on the way when he quickly says. "Oh and uh she hasn't seen anything except the castle and that's it your highness."

"Ok dear. Now go along!" She orders him out of the room. "Come back in an hour!"

He closes the door and we hear his foot steps fade away out of the hallway.

"Ahh. He's probably not going to Art's room. He and Art have a history together." She explains looking at the door.

"Is it Art or Arther and you just call him Art?" I ask.

She looks and me and says, "No, just Art. I wanted a unique name for him, and my husband wanted Arther so we decided to shorten it to Art."

"Ok.........ummm can you answer a few questions for me please?"

"No, not right now. We need to get down to business because you guys where slow getting here and I have a Light coming to meet me in an hour. So let's talk about Elementa." She says leading me to her two comfy chairs infront of her desk and she then goes to the one elegant chair behind her desk.

"So Elementa is like our country. Externila is in the middle of everything because it's where the castle is. Also Externila is a circle. All the places are a circle. We then have the six surrounding cities. There are Ux, Frix, Trabik, Maston, Axy, and Wis. We then have our Natural Habitats surrounding the cities. Usually pure Waters live in Wastan, pure Winds live in Winzon, pure Earths live in Ealthia, pure Lights live in Listion, pure Fires live in Fitren, and pure Darknesses live in Dagon. Not all pure Elementals live in their natural habitats. Some live in the normal cities and some Elementals with two different Elemental parents live their. Although you have to have that element. Sorry about the explaining but you kind of have to know this before you begin your studies at Aspen Academy, which is also in Externilia." Queen Bee explains pointing at a map behind her desk. She points at each circle while explaining to me.

"So do you have that?" She asks me.

"Yes. Is that all I need to know right now?" I ask.

"I think so, you will learn a lot at Aspen-oh wait, so all the Elementals that do their education go to Aspen. It is a huge school. Has 8 floors, one for every level and an extra one for offices, the gym, and extra classes. You normally start when you are 11 at Year 1. And since you are-wait how old are you?" She asks interrupting herself.

"Umm....I'm 14." I say shyly.

"Oh. Umm.... huh, ok. Well we can put you into Year 4. Well first let's see what you can do and that will actually determine what year we place you in. This normally doesn't happen. You have to be 11 to go into Year 1 and if you aren't you can't be in Year 1 that year. So let's see if I have to make some changes for you." She says with a smile while encouraging me to do something with my Water.

I stand up and notice she had a huge aquarium in her wall. I walk over and grab some water. I also grab some from the air. I start to form it into a platform. I then start to step on it when the Queen stands up from her chair.

"Keep going I just want to see." She tells me,

I keep going and soon I am standing on water. I laugh a little and I try something I have never done before. I start to move the water platform with me on it. I start off slowly but I soon get faster and faster.

"How!!" The Queen exclaims.

"I don't know!" I laugh.

I then come to a stop in front Queen Bee. I step of and grab the water, feeling it was over my hands smoothly. I then turn it into a fish and place it into the fish tank. I make the fish move and all the normal fish get scared and swim to their little places. I step back admiring my work when Queen Bee speaks.

"How did you learn that?" She asks saying the same thing Jayden said, making me jump and loose concentration to the fish. The water fish turns back into normal water.

"Learned it myself." I say a little to proudly.

"You can't have just learned that yourself. That is super advanced Element skill. Only the strongest Waters know how to do that." She tells me.

I stay silent because I don't know what to say but good thing she moves to her desk and says, "I'll put you in Year 4. You seem like you belong there."

"Ok, is that all?" I ask.

"Yes I think so. Jayden should be coming soon to escort you to your room. You can ask him anything he should know the answers."

"Ok-" I start to say but I get interrupted by a person coming through the door.

"Queen Bee, I have been waiting out there for five minutes now, so are you done?" Asks a preppy voice that has bullied me my whole junior high experience.

I turn around to be met with those piercing ice blue eyes again.

Hazel Copper.

How!!!! I thought when I came here I wouldn't see her ever again and now she is here!!!! And how is she an Elemental!!! I scream to myself.

"Ah..sorry Hazel. I was just seeing Madilyn. She is new here and I was just about done here. And we are waiting for Jayden to come back to escort her to her room." Queen Bee tells her.

"Oh don't worry. I can escort her. Jayden has some business to attend to." Hazel says starting to grab my hand.

"Do you know where her room is?" The Queen asks.

"Yes. I got it from my boyfriend."

Hazel is Jayden's girlfriend??? I question.

"Ok." The Queen says. "Come right back after so we can talk."

"Ok." Hazel says to her.

I have no choice but follow Hazel.

She leads me down the Royal corridor and starts to lead me down the 11 flights of stairs. But once we get down to the main level we keep going down into what looks like the basement.

"I don't think the Queen would put my room down here. There isn't even doors." I tell Hazel. She then stops in her tracks and looks into my eyes.

"I know way more than you, and you will not question my knowledge. I have been looking for you when I was placed in the human world by him. I was instructed to find you and bring you to him. I had no idea you would be the person I was looking for. I new I was looking for a Madilyn so I kept a close eye on you, but when you sprayed water at my poor boyfriend, Jayden, I new it was you. But he got to you first and took you here. Not to him. I was instructed to do something then leave you and come back later for you because he isn't ready yet." She tells me dragging me down the dark hallway with a death grip on my wrist. We reach a dark corner and she starts to punch me.

What did I do? I think trying to rack my brain for anything I did to her. *And what is up with him?*

She keeps punching and kicking me. I try to fight back and I end up getting a few hits on her before she pins me down and starts to hit my face.

"Stop!!" I try to yell. I end up reaching my hand up and pulling out some of her hair. She cries in pain but doesn't stop.

"No. I am doing it for him. He needs this and once he gets the satisfaction he will be proud of me and award me." She says still punching me.

I scream and scream. But no one comes to save me. Just her punching me and my worthless screams.

I start to see stars and soon she is off of me and throwing me into the corner. I start to black out when I here her voice close to me.

"You deserved this for what you mother did." She says.

What?

Then everything goes black.

Six

"What happened?" Says an accented voice.

"I don't know?" Says a high pitched voice. "I let her go with Hazel and then my guards come to me saying they're hearing screams come from the basement. I tell them to go and check and two different guards bring her to me. No one was in sight. I have no idea how she got there or why."

"What about Hazel?" The accented voice says.

"Jayden, come on. Hazel wouldn't do this. She is my niece and I trust her. So if you would excuse me. I am going to go and check on something." With that, a door slams shut. I feel another presence in the room and it must be Jayden.

"You wouldn't understand." Jayden says under his breath and he leaves too.

It's dead silent and it feels uncomfortable. I try to open my eyes. They are heavy but I am able to open them. I'm staring at a huge room. It has a giant blue canopy bed in the middle which, I am laying on. There is a big window on the other side of the room, with a seat attached to it. There is a sofa near the wall to my left and double doors to me right. I would guess that is the exit to the hallway. Next to the sofa is another set of double doors, but smaller than the others. They are probably the closet doors. There is a bookshelf by the window with tons of books on it.

Good. I think to myself. Books are my life.

Next to the book selves is a huge desk made of dark wood. Next there are three dressers around the room for clothes.

Who needs so much clothes? I ask myself.

Next to the bed, are two bedside tables next to it. Next to dresser #2 is a full length mirror. I am to busy looking at the room I miss the knock on the door. It's only when there is a harder one I notice it.

"Come in." I say.

"Hello?" Says a shy voice.

"Hi." I say to a girl coming in. She is about my age with white hair that is in a loose bun and clear sparkly eyes. She has on black glasses that pop against her light skin and hair. She has on a blue dress that goes down to her knees and she has silver flats.

"I'm Winter Feral. I am a Wind." The girl tells me. "You must be Madilyn. Half the Castle is worried about you because no one knows who did it except you and we have never had anything like this happen."

"Oh ummm......" I trail off.

"Sorry if I am being rude but I brought food." She says holding out a tray full of mouth watering foods. "Would you mind telling me who did this. Jayden is angry and he wants to kill who did this. And you never want to see him angry. Ok, well maybe he doesn't really want to kill the person because when he is, he is a super softy."

"Well ummm.......Haze-" I didn't even finish her name when Winter jumps up.

"I knew it. Jayden knew it. The Queen doesn't. Hazel is the Queens niece and she believes anything that is against Hazel because Hazel is the closest thing to a daughter she has ever had!!! She has always wanted a daughter but got stuck with Art. Everyone has noticed how terrible she is to him." She rambles. "I knew it. Jayden is going to kill her-wait Hazel is his girlfriend. How? What? Why?" She questions herself.

"Well ummm....Hazel was my bully in junior high and I never thought she was an Elemental. But she did say some weird things. Also did some weird things, like punching and kicking me." I tell Winter.

"Tell me!" Winter pleads. But before I could get any words out Jayden and the Queen come barging in the room, followed my Aaron and Art. They all seem to be arguing over something.

"She's awake!!" The Queen announces to everyone, making everyone stop their bickering. "Winter you may go!" The Queen urges Winter out. Winter looks taken aback but soon dismisses it and starts to leave.

"No!" Says a voice. Everyone looks at me, even Winter, and that's when I realized I said those words.

"Excuse me?" The Queen says.

"No. Winter stays. She brought me food. She stays." I say proudly. Aaron is shaking his head in approval, Art is looking at Winter and I with disgust, the Queen is just plain out confused, Winter turned to look at me with appreciation in her eyes, and Jayden is.........well he looks like he wants to rip someone's throat out. He keeps looking at me. I have to look away quick because I feel my face getting red.

Why emotions? Why now?

"You don't run things here new girl so Winter is getting out whether you like it or not!" All eyes turn to Art, who is pointing a finger at me.

"Who is hurt here?" I challenge. Art looks taken aback at what I said. "Winter stays."

"Fine." Art says stepping back.

"Madilyn knows who attacked her!" Winter says to everyone, forgetting that I just aloud her to stay.

"Who!!" Says the Queen enthusiastically,

I look at Jayden and say, "Your girlfriend. Hazel." Everyone looks at me confused. Jayden has pure hatred plastered on his face. He turns his face away from mine and walks over to the window and just staring out into the distance.

"Hazel would never do such a thing!" The Queen exclaims. "She is like my daughter and would never!"

"She kept talking about him." I say. "She wouldn't stop. It was her job to beat me up. She then said I deserved it because of what my mother did. And I don't even know if Poppy is my mom or some other mysterious person is?"

Everyone looks at me weirdly.

"Would you like to see your parents one last time?" A voice asks. We all turn to Jayden, who is still standing by the window. He turns his eyes to me and looks at me with a lot of caring in his blazing eyes.

"Yes." I say.

"You absolutely can't!" The Queen shouts.

"Yes she can. She has the right. She was pulled from her home with nothing. If you where in her shoes, you would want to go visit them one last time, right?" Jayden asks the Queen, walking over to her.

"Fine. Only once." The Queen orders. "Everyone out. Let her rest."
Everyone starts to leave and once everyone is out I notice Jayden
is still here.

"Uhhhh.....how can I help you?" I joke.

"Even when hurt you crack a joke." He chuckles. "Oh and your
injures are, a bruised back, one cracked rib, marks on your face
and a bruised nose. Nothing to bad except the rib. We had Eriok
come in and run water over you to help you heal faster. You are
pretty much healed except Eriok wants you not to do anything that
physical today. Tomorrow you can."

"Thx. And who is Eriok?" I question.

"He is one of our castle healers. We have a set of healers for each
element and he is a water." He tells me. He looks away thinking
and then out of nowhere he asks. "Was it really Hazel?"

"Yes. How did she bribe you into letting her take me?" I question
him.

"Well first I waited outside the Queens door and then I decided I'll
go and get a snack because the meeting was taking an hour. When
I got there I saw Hazel. She was looking evil as ever and she was
talking to Art, which probably wasn't good. She then came over
and told me she can take you to your room. I wasn't sure and I
protested but she said she had to go to the Queen after and so I
allowed her. After I was down on the main floor walking around
because I had nothing to do, I saw her take you down into the
basement but I thought nothing of it because I thought you guys
where doing a secret girl thing. Stupid mistake on my part. But
then I was going to go to help with some work Aaron had because
I was bored, I heard some screams. I told the guards, some went to

the Queen and some went to see who it was. We came down and saw you unconscious. We took you to the Queen and she told to put you in your room. And then the Queen and I had an argument of who did it. When I was down there I saw Hazel's hair in you hands, but I didn't see her. She must have escaped before we came down. But I knew exactly it was her." He explains to me, "And before you ask. No. Hazel and I are not boyfriend and girlfriend. Everyone thinks we are but we aren't. We were until she betrayed Elementa. I have hated her and never trusted her since. Now tell me your side."

I start to tell him and he listens intently to my side. Once I finish he chuckles.

"I knew it."

"Knew what?" I ask curiously.

"Poppy is actually your mother. Or should I say Christin Waker. You don't have a second mom, Madilyn."

"What do you mean?" I ask confused.

"She is an Elemental. And she took you to the human world. She is a traitor like Hazel."

Seven

I can't speak. My throat is dry and Jayden has that look in his eye that is saying, *speak!!!*

"Huh........" Is all I can muster.

"Madilyn, are you ok with this info?" Jayden asks.

"Ya. It's just why didn't my mother tell me?" I ask starting to tear up. "She was the only one like me among the humans and she didn't tell me. Why is she even a mother!!" I scream.

"Hey! Don't get worked up. You love her." Jayden reassures me.

"Nooo!!!" I scream at him while throwing a pillow at the wall. It misses terribly but whatever.

"How's the Mad Dog doin' in here?" Aaron says while entering the door with Winter not far behind. I give him the best glare I can muster.

"A, this might not be the best time." Jayden says to Aaron who looks like he is about to disobey.

"She's fine. She just needs an Aaron in her life." He jokes.

"Get out!!" I scream, throwing another pillow. This time at him. He catches it and says, "10 points for The Mad Dog!!!"

"Madi, what's wrong?" Winter asks in a innocent voice. She walks to the side of the bed, grabs the tray of food, brings it to the desk, and walks back for the bed and sits down.

"Her mother." Jayden's butts in before I can say anything. "She was an Elemental and never told Madi. She's mad right now."

"I am not!!" I yell at him, throwing another pillow at him. He caught it of course.

"20 points!!!" Aaron yells from a chair that I didn't know I had in my room. We all glare at him and he glares back but ends up cracking up and we just ignore him.

"Hey don't ignore meeeee!!!!" He yells at us. We still do.

"Waaa!! Guys. Aren't we friends??? He asks sliding of the chair like a five year old.

"Dude, shut up!" Jayden tells him while throwing a pillow at him.

"Oh it's on!!" Aaron yells, throwing a pillow at Jayden. Jayden gets another pillow from behind me and chucks it at Aaron. They continue throwing until suddenly I have an urge to throw something to. I stand up ignoring my rib. I grab a pillow and throw it as hard as I can. It hits Jayden strait in the back of the head. He doesn't expects it, and he trips over the soft baby blue carpet at the foot of my bed, I didn't know was there. He lands face first into the carpet.

Winter laughs hysterically.

"Ow." He says flatly. "Aaron you gunna get it now!!!" He yells into the carpet while flailing his arms around. He doesn't make an effort to get up yet.

"T-that wasn't me-e." Stutters Aaron looking terrified. He puts his hands up while dropping the pillow.

"You gunna get it!" He whisper-yells to me.

"Oh I know it was you!!" Jayden yells into the carpet. "You know Madilyn. This is an awesome carpet."

"Umm..ok."

"Get up Jay. We need to continue!!" Winter says still laughing while trying to lift him up. It looks like he is making himself heavy on purpose. "Get up!!!!!!" We all try to lift Jayden up. We give up and secretly communicate that we are going to drop him on the count of three.

We start to count silently.

"1." We mouth.

"2." We whisper.

"3!" We yell.

We drop him onto the carpet. He screams like a baby on his trip to the floor.

"You know we have school tomorrow? Right?" He asks.

"Hehe!" We say and then we burst out laughing. Full on, people on the ground, tears in our eyes and clutching our stomachs. Jayden obviously doesn't join in. He actually sits up and glares at us as we laugh our butts of. He gets up and walks to the door.

"Bu-bye!!!!!" He yells.

"Noooo. J.J. Come back!!" Aaron cries.

"J.J.?" I question.

"Ya. Baby name."

"I've told you before to not call me that, Grumpy Gorge!" Jayden yells, but before he has a time to shut the door, Aaron gets up and grabs another pillow. He dashes to the door and hits Jayden square in the jaw. I just realized how many pillows I actually have.

"OWWWW!!! Why is everyone attacking me!!!" He shouts while we laugh. "I'm gunna have a bruise tomorrow and that's not going to be good, guys!" He stares at us. "Shut up."

W-weee.......ca-an't!!!! Your t-o-o fun-ny when a-ngryyyyy!!!!!" Winter tries to say between fits of laughter. Jayden shuts the door and we just keep laughing.

"He's angry!" Aaron says. "Right Madilyn!"

"Ya!! And you know, I don't mind Madi, right? And what is up with Grumpy Gorge?? Like seriously?"

"Weeeeeell, when we where is Year 1, Hazel and Art nicknamed me Grumpy Gorge because I was always grumpy. That's also why now I make jokes, but.........Gorge was actually the Headmaster of our school and he was super grumpy.......so that's why they nicknamed me Grumpy Gorge. It stuck of course. It actually stopped in Year 5 but now Jayden uses it as an insult. So never ever call me Grumpy Gorge, Mad dog!" He says pointing a finger at me.

"Seriously, Aaron!!" I say smacking him with a pillow. We start to run around the room hitting each other with pillows when we hear the door open.

"Well you don't seem hurt anymore." Says a voice. We turn to see Art smirking and leaning on the door frame. I quickly fall to the floor with my hand on my forehead.

"Oh, help me Art. I'm hurt!" I laugh.

"Very funny. Now get up and come with me."

"Why does she have to go with youuuuu???" Aaron asks him.

"Madilyn, come now." He orders.

I don' t move from my spot because I just realized how sore my muscles are and my back aches from falling on the floor. So does my ribs.

"I don't wanna!!" I say like a baby.

"Come!" He yells.

I sit up in a pouting position with my arms over my chest and flatly say, "No."

He sighs and leaves. But before he shuts the door he turns around and tells me, "You will regret not coming with me today. Have a nice rest of your day and I'll see you tomorrow at school." With that he shuts the door and we all burst out laughing.

"We totally pissed him off!" Winter says. She looks so pretty even laughing.

"Ok, well we should go and get ready for school tomorrow. I'll come by tomorrow and help you get to you classes." Winter says, pulling Aaron with her. "Oh and you and I are in the same grade. Jayden, Aaron, and Art are all two years above us."

"Ok. Thank you." I say and with that they are out of the room.

I sit on the floor for a while absorbed in my thoughts. I soon snap out of it and climb onto my bed. I fall asleep peacefully for the first time in forever.

•*•*•

I was walking through a hallway. That was covered in nothing. Had no windows, doors, paintings, nothing. I don't know where this hallway is, when, all of a sudden, there is a cold chill going down my spin. I turn around and see a black shadow at the other end of the hall. I start to turn around and run when a wall is suddenly at my back.

"What? When did this get here?"

I spin around to face the Shadow again. The thing is moving closer. I try to run but the wall is in my way.

"Come here little one!" The Shadows voice says. His voice is like layers of darkness pressing onto me.

"No!!" I yell. I can barley get the words out. My voice is heavy from the layers of darkness he has put on me.

He slithers toward me. His wall seams to be moving closer to him. So soon we will be close together and I will have no where to run.

"Come here!" The creepy voice orders.

"Ahh!" I try to yell. All the layers of darkness is pressing on me and I can barley talk. I try to push them off me. It helps a little but not much.

I was trying to much and the layers of darkness pressing on me. I was to busy falling to the floor, I didn't register that a hand was picking me up.

"Get off me!!" I mumble.

The thing points me toward it, making me look into a cape. I don't see anything. I keep searching for eyes but there are non. I was to busy looking for eyes or a face at all, I didn't realize I was being held by this person or thing. I realize to late, because when I try to kick the thing of me. They pull me closer and whisper into my ear.

"You will pay for what your mother did to me!" He whispers. He then let's me go and I scream, scream and scream.

I shoot up from my bed screaming and looking around the room. The room is blurry and that's when I realize I am crying. I cry and cry not stopping. When it gets to around 4 o'clock, I start to here people roaming around the castle and that is when I fall asleep.

.*.*.

"Wake up sleepy head!" Screams a voice right into my ear.

"I don't wanna!" I whine.

"Well it's your first day of school and that isn't going to be nice if you missed it."

"Moooooooom, I don't wanna!" I whine even more.

"Seriously? You think I'm your mom. I'm Winter!" She screams into my ear making me fall of the bed.

"Wow, ok. You don't have to scream into my ear Winter." I tell her.

"Well then get up and get ready. You uniform is on the couch." She tells me and walks out of the room, "and don't go back to sleep!"

"You sound just like my mom!" I yell back.

"Okaaaaaaay!!" She yells back.

I start to get up when I feel a chill go down my spin.

Why? I thought I was free!!! I complain in my head.

I look around the room and see nothing. I get a glimpse of the dark hallway when I blink.

"What? I'm awake. This can't be happening!" I yell.

I start to look for the Shadow when I am grabbed by the neck and lifted of the floor. I try to scream but the shadow whispers, "You scream, and every Water dies , everything gets crushes, and it all turns to rumble right before you." Before I can even get a peep out.

I stop struggling and look into the Shadows eyes. Instead of seeing pure darkness, I see eyes this time. But pure black that are filed with hatred and death. I am suddenly dropped to the floor with a hard thud. The shadow is gone and my neck is throbbing. I didn't notice how hard my neck was being held. I rub it and feel a liquid running down my fingers. I take my fingers away from my neck and see red staining my fingers. I run to the bathroom and look at my neck. There are finger nail imprints witch the blood is coming from.

"Darn. How am I going to go to the Academy now. Hopefully I didn't get it on their clothes they let me borrow." I say out loud.

I clean off the blood and put bandages over the wounds. I then decide to look at my rib. I lift up my shirt and see a bruise that is almost healed.

"Ouch." I say. I decide to ignore it because I have bigger things to do. I walk across the huge bedroom to the closet doors. When I am passing the area where the strange Shadow person picked me up, I feel chills and quickly run to the closet. I open the doors and am met by so much clothes.

Wait. Didn't Winter say she left my clothes on the couch? I think while looking at the couch, and sure enough my uniform is right there.

"Great they aren't going to cover up the bandages."

I walk over and try the uniform on and if fits quit well. Not to snug but not to big. There is a grey skirt that is shorter than my knees. A white top that is short sleeved with a navy blue cardigan that goes over. Over the heart on both pieces there is a fox, strong and fierce. A blue tie ties around my neck. I'm examining the uniform, I jump when someone speaks.

"Uhm......." Says a voice. I whirl around and am met by those blazing orange eyes. I look down in embarrassment and I feel my face heating up.

"Sorry I didn't see you there." I say awkwardly, blushing.

"No, no." He says coming closer. "You look good in that uniform. And Winter told me to come and get you." He informs me. He has on the same uniform except pants and not a skirt and he has a forest green cardigan instead of a navy blue. His crest over his heart on both his white shirt and cardigan is a panda having it's back to us and turning it's head to face the world.

"Why do you have a different crest and coloured uniform. Do you go to a secret school I don't know about?" I ask.

"Haha. Your funny. No I do not go to a secret school. Every grade level has their own animal. Year 6's are pandas. Yes we do use Elementless animals." He explains to me.

"What are the Elementless?"

"Oh ya. Sorry I forgot you are still learning our terms . The Elementless are simply what you call them, humans. We say Elementless because they don't have any elements." He explains to me. "So are you ready to go now?"

"Yes. Sorry. Let's go."

Eight

We are standing in front of a five story building with two buildings beside it with two more stories. It has crystals built into it with all the elements. It has Aspen Academy written in big letters above the front door. It was also mainly windows.

"Whoa....." I trail off.

"Right? Isn't it beautiful?" Jayden asks me.

"Yes. Really pretty. I love it!" I exclaim.

"So on the left building is Year 1 and 2. Year 1 is on the bottom and 2 is on the top. In the middle building is the main floor,3,4,5, and the offices and other extra classrooms. The main floor is on the bottom and that is usually where students go and hang out or do last minute homework. Then Year 3 is on top of that, then 4, and 5. Then on top of those are the extra classroom and offices. Next the last building to your right is Year 6 and 7. And the order goes the same as the other buildings. Year 6 on the bottom and Year 7 on the top." He explains to me, pointing to each building while talking. "Sadly we won't see each other during school, except lunch, because I'll be in the right wing and you'll be in the middle wing."

"Oh. Where is the cafeteria?" I ask.

"The what?" He asks confused.

"The eating palace." I say in a duh tone.

"Ohhhhhhh, I don't think we have a proper name but it's a separate building behind the middle wing. Of course it is connected to the building but it's it own building. Then the Combat training is behind all the buildings beside the forest. Oh and what's with the bandages on you neck?" He questions while pointing to my bandages. I step back, covering my neck with my hands. "No seriously, let me see. I can't let Hazel get to you!"

"It wasn't Hazel!" I say while stepping back again as he steps forward.

"Then who was it?" He demands.

"If I tell you, you'd think I'm crazy."

"No I wouldn't. Now tell me and show me!" He orders.

"Fine. I had this dream, well I don't know if it's a dream anymore, with this Shadow and a hallway. The Shadow whispered the same thing as Hazel did in my ear. I woke up crying and then at around 4:00 I finally went to sleep." I explain while removing my hands. "And then after when Winter came in to wake me up, I felt a chill by my bed and then the Shadow came and actually picked me up and told me some really bad things."

"What where the things he told you?" He questions while looking at my wounds.

"Well-"

"Jay!" Aaron panicky yells.

"What Aaron?" Jayden asks, turning his attention to Aaron.

"Another Water is in the Hospital!" He says urgently. "And it's Quinn!"

"Quinn!" Jayden says panicked.

Another Water is in their hospital? The Shadow said that if I scream, all the Waters will die! I think nervously.

"Who's Quinn?" I ask. They both look at me obviously forgetting I was standing right here.

"Quinn is in Year 7 and she is actually the strongest girl Water. We have a strongest girl and boy for each element. And Quinn is the strongest girl Water. Also the strongest Water in the school. She is super nice, kind and gentle. Everyone wants to be around her. And since Waters have been going to the Emergency Healings with poisoning, the Waters have actually been dying with the poisoning. We don't want Quinn to die, or any of the other Waters. Because if we lose an Element for good, we won't be in good shape. And hopefully you don't go either." Jayden explains to me.

"You ok?" Aaron asks noticing my silence and my facial expression.

"Well the Shadow actually said that the Waters will die before my eyes." I tell them. Aaron looks confused and Jayden is surprised.

"Are you sure?" Jayden asks nervously.

"Yes. I am sure."

"Guys are you coming? Classes are about to start!" We all turn to see Winter coming towards us in her uniform. She has her hair in a

high ponytail with some of her hair hanging by her face, framing
it. She is carrying a book bag which is overflowing with books and
she even has more in her arms.

"We will but we actually need to talk to the Queen because
Madilyn gave us some important information." Jayden says to her.

"Well sorry you can't because my mom is on some business in
Wastan. So you are going to have to wait. And for you Madilyn,
Wastan is the Water habitat." Art says unexpectedly, coming up
behind us. He has on his forest green uniform which he look super
cute in. His pale yellow hair is styled messy and that makes him
super cute.

"Can't you stay out of things Art?" Aaron asks.

"No. Because I'm the Queen's son so I am respected. And it's my
job to see how the school is going and I have to always butt into
your conversations."

"That doesn't make sense?" I say.

He looks at me and glares. "Stop being the smart new girl. You
just got here and you don't understand a thing!" He says angrily.

"Well can we break this up and get into the school and get to our
classes!" Winter says a little agitated.

"Fine." Art says as he starts to walk away. "Oh Madilyn, I'll see
you later and tell your friends to stay out of the Queen's business."
With that he walks into the school.

"Wow I hate him!" Winter says angrily. We all turn to look at her. "What?" She says and storms off into the building.

"Well I guess we are going to have to wait until she is free to tell her." Jayden says. "Madilyn come on. I have to bring you to meet Dean Huckle." He says taking my hand.

"Wait. Aaron said it was Principal Gorge?" I say confused.

"Well actually the only reason I am not Grumpy Gorge anymore is because he died. He was a Water and he died because of the poisonous water. So now it is Dean Huckle. And never call her Huckleberry. She hates it because it isn't her name." Aaron explains to me. "I've gotten on her bad side for saying it." He whispers to me, making me laugh.

"Come now we are going to meet her." Jayden tugs me along through the huge class front doors with Aaron trailing along. We barley make it anywhere before loud sirens go off.

"What's going on?" I shout. Instead of answering Jayden grabs my wrist and shoves my sleeve up my arm.

"What is it?" I try to shout over the ear piercing sound.

"Come!!" He orders as he drags me back out the doors. Before I leave I see Aaron standing by the door confused.

"What's going on?" I demand.

"You aren't marked." He shows me my wrist. Then he grabs his wrist and shows it to me. On his wrist is a small flame. "When you are born you get this mark to tell everyone what element you are.

And it has special features in it so a highly protected building, like the Academy, can sense who is coming in that is supposed to and who isn't. You don't have it because we forgot to mark you. And that is why those sirens went off." He is just done explaining when a guy walks out.

"Mr. MaZinn. Who would you bring into the school that isn't supposed to?" He asks in a deep voice. This guy has light brown hair that is in a low man bun. His ice blue eyes are filled with confusion and a little anger. He has on a robe that is a mix of light and dark blue. Brown pants stick out from the bottom and polished black shoes cover his feet.

"Sorry Weltar. This is Madilyn Evans and she is new here. The Queen has ordered her to attend and we totally forgot to mark her. She is a Water and she can prove it." Jayden tells him.

"Show me!!" Welter orders, nodding his head to me. I move my hands up and down, nervous to not follow this guys order. I grab the moister from the air and start to form it into the platform again like I did in Queen Bee's office.

"Step on it!" He orders me. I easily step on it. And when he is about to open his mouth I move the plateform. I keep going higher and higher. I am about the third story when, without warning the platform gives way. I fall to the ground but before I get passed Welters 6'5 form I create another platform that stops my fall. I slowly lower myself to the ground and let the water go back to the air.

"Well clearly she is a Water. But she needs to be marked. Go ask the Dean if she is allowed to go around the school without a mark and then if she is allowed. Right after school is finished get her marked!" He order Jayden. "You may go to her now." Welter turns on his heel and walks into the building. We follow him and this time the sirens don't go off.

"I turned them off." We turn to see Aaron smiling on the right.

"Thanks, but we really have to go see Dean Huckle. See you." Jayden says to Aaron.

We have walked into what looks like a main area where students sit and hang out. A lot of student are looking at us but soon go back to their work. There is an elegant water fountain in the middle spraying water in a fancy way. Benches are scattering the area with students already sitting at them. Against the walls are tables covered in students doing last minute homework. There are two hallways facing each other. And a staircase behind the fountain. We walk around the fountain and up the stairs. We are met by a fake Tiger ready to pounce. We are also met by a hallway with a bunch of doors. There are more hallways leading to other classrooms filled with lockers on both sides, as we walk to another set of stairs on the opposite side of where we came from. We then go up to Year 4.

"This is your level. You'll be here for the most part." Jayden explains to me. We walk past the Strong fox and down the identical hallway to the other set of stairs leading to Year 5, when we are stopped short by a girl with flaming orange hair fading into yellow. Her left eyes is red and the other one is black. She has a scar down her left eye that makes her look super mean. She is at least two feet taller than me, but smaller than Jayden. She also has on a the same uniform as me.

I'm guesting she is in my Year. I think to myself.

"Dawn. If you where to excuse us. I half to take Madilyn to Dean Huckle." Jayden says to this Dawn person.

"J.J. Come on. You need to work on your training for you Element. It's not going to get better by just sitting around." Dawn says.

"Dawn. I seriously can't. I wish I could but I can't. I'll catch you later." With that he drags me to the flight of stairs that brings us to the Year 5 floor.

"Sorry. She's my cousin and she is attached to me. We have the same Element so it's easy for us to bond." He explains. We have now reached the bottom of the stairs that go to the last floor in the huge building.

"This is where the Dean's office is. And classrooms for super powerful Elementals. So watch out." He then tugs me up the stairs. "It is almost identical to the last three floors. Except the classrooms are a little bigger." We have now reached the end of the hallway. And instead of a staircase it is a door.

"Now let me tell you. Dean Huckle is a Darkness Element. She is super strong. She can press layers of darkness on you and you couldn't move for a week. So never get on her bad side." He explains to me.

"Ok." I say. Jayden turns around and knocks on the door. We wait for a few second and then he knocks again.

"Huh?" He says. He tries to knock again and silence. We keep waiting and knocking but obviously no one is coming to the door.

"Dean Huckle. Are you in there?" Jayden questions as he opens the door. He steps in first and gasps. I move forward and knock him out of the way. My curious side getting the better of me.

"Madi-" He starts but I put my hand up to silence him. I see nothing but I sense something. It's dark and mysterious. I feel it's presence in here.

"What's going on?" Jayden whispers from the door. I ignore him and keep walking straight. The office has a huge desk in the middle covered in papers and other silly things. The circled walls are covered in selves. Not one space of the walls are showing. On the floor is a white fluffy carpet. On the carpet are two black leather chairs and behind the desk is the most fancy chair I have ever seen.

I keep walking until I am standing beside the desk.

"I know your here." I whisper.

"What did you say?" Jayden asks. But I don't have time to respond because something knocks me to the floor. I cringe at my other injuries but shake it off, focused on the thing tackling me. I see stars clouding my vision but not letting this thing get to me.

"I will make you pay!!!" The voice yells into my ear. The darkness presses on me but I force it back up towards the thing on me. I fight with all my might and as soon as it's started I am laying on the carpet breathing heavily.

"Madilyn!!" Jayden yells coming toward me, panicked helping me up.

"I'm fine Jayden. I'm fine." I reacher him.

"No you are not. This black thing was all over you. How did it get in here?" He wonders to himself. I point to the slightly cracked open window I just noticed now. He gets up and walks over and let's out a ear splitting scream. I stand up in an instant, a little wobbly but I keep moving. I make it to the window and there on the ground, splattered on the grass is a woman. She has black hair splattered on the grass and her face. Her black lifeless eyes stare deathly at us and all we can do is stare back at her.

"Who is that?" I wonder. I'm shocked at what I see, I don't register the person entering the room.

"Dean Huckle." A voice says. Jayden and I turn to see Art, standing against the door frame smirking.

Nine

I stare at him blankly.

Hoe does he know??? I question myself. *Did he do this??*

"You did this didn't you!" I acuse him. He looks taken aback at my sudden out burst.

"No. I did not. I just found her when I came in here earlier. I haven't said anything to anyone because it would be chaos with the Waters and Dean Huckle, a Dark, dying. So I think you, Jayden and I should keep our mouths shut. Say Dean Huckle is ill for now. Welter or Injie can take over for now."

"N-" I start to protest but he quickly cuts me off.

"One day I will be King and you listen to what I say. Because I can sentenced you to death." He orders me while looking deathly at me.

I stare at him shocked. He stares at me for what feel like eternity and I get uncomfortable so I decide to speak.

"Well that's a little excessive." I tell him. It only angers him more and soon he grabs me and slams me on Dean Huckles desk.

"Art!! What are you-stooop!!" I interrupt myself because he keeps slamming me on the desk. Papers are flying everywhere and Dean Huckles belongings fall to the floor. She has a lamp on her desk and that falls in my face. It doesn't do to much but enough to make me scream.

"Owwww!!!" I scream in agony.

"Art, get off her!" Jayden orders. Art turns to see Jayden, obviously forgetting he was in the room and watching this whole thing.

"She deserves this. She keeps stepping out of line and someone has to teach her!" Art informs Jayden. Jayden just gets more angry and starts to yell.

"She just got here yesterday and has been attacked twice now! She is still learning and she won't be perfect! Nobody is! It's time you learn that Art! And Madilyn will step out of line and now it's acceptable and soon it won't, but now she just got here and give her a rest ok Art. Also you are a Light and Queen Bee's son. You have to learn some self control!!!" Jayden yells heating up. He looks like he is going to explode. He storms out the room slamming the door closed. It just pops back open by the force.

"He wishes he was me." Art turns to me. He looks into my eyes weirdly. I step back but that just makes him step closer.

"Art. Don't hurt me." I plead.

"Well, then stop stepping out of line!" He orders as he steps closer. I keep stepping back until my back is against a bookshelf. I bump into it so hard the bookshelf I have bumped into starts to tip. Art steps back smirking. I am frozen to even move. I realize to late, I start to run away but something pushes me back. I see Art pushing light against me, keeping me in the zone of the falling bookshelf. All I can think to do is duck. I wrap my arms around myself in terror.

"Get out from there!!" A deep voice yells to me a second later. I look up and see a boy wearing the Year 4 uniform. He has slick black hair with bangs that fall over his black eyes that have a hint of blue to them. He has freckles splattered on his face like confetti. He has a deep scar across his left eyebrow that makes him look dangerous and daring. He has one hand pointed at me and the other at Art, covering him in a shield of black.

He must be a Dark. I think to myself. Using the term Art said.

I look up to see the boy holding the bookshelf with darkness.

"For goodness sake get the hell outa there!" He yells to me. I scramble my way to his side and he turns both his hands to Art.

"Don't do anything to her and I'll let you go!" He shouts to Art.

"No! When I'm free, instead of punishing her I'll punish you by executing you for keeping me hostage!!" Art shouts. His shouts are a little muffled because of the darkness shield. He doesn't even try to break out of the shield. He looks way to confident.

"I thought we don't do that anymore!!" The boy shouts back to Art.

"Well, when I am King I'll make sure it's back in place!!" Art shouts.

"Well right now you're not King!! Queen Bee took the execution away because it was happening to much with her father!! So you can't execute me because you're not king!!" The boy shouts, his hair wildly flapping around. Art seems at a loss for words. Instead of firing an insult back he slumps to the floor, while the shield shrinks closer to him and thickens up. Art wraps his arms around himself and closes his eyes. I was just thinking he had passed out or given up when something explodes. A bright light blinds me and I am sent flying back towards the door along with bangs boy. He smashes into the frame, when I go through the door.

"Madilyn!!" I hear someone calling my name but can't figure out who. I fly down the hall and suddenly smash into stone.

"Argh!" I grunt and blood shoots from my mouth and nose. I fall down onto the stairs below me. I tumble all the way to the bottom and about to black out. But before I have a chance to fall into unconsciousness I see those orange eyes staring back at me, concerned.

Ten

I struggle to make my eyelids move but they end up giving in.

Wow. Not even two days in and I am already the victim! I think to myself sarcastically. I try to move but everything aches. Instead of trying to move I calm myself and look around. I am lying in a very uncomfortable bed with curtains to the side. There are more beds lined up like mine on both sides of the room. The room has bottles on shelves and other weird potion things. I notice a door on one end of the room and double doors on the other. On the other side of the one door I hear muffled talking.

"This isn't like Elementa!" Says a voice I don't recognize.

"We know. We are trying to figure out where the poison is coming from and killing Waters." Says a high pitched voice.

"Well my crew and I are trying to figure out what's happening and we have others trying to cure it. It's going very slow and I don't think we can stop it. So far we have collected some data from the dead Waters. The poison seems to be coursing through their body, starting at their hands and making it to their heart. We don't know how to get it because we don't know where the poison actually is because it's invisible, Queen. We need your help too. You are the Queen." The voice says to Queen Bee.

"I am trying. I have visited Wasten and investigated but there is no sign of poison yet there." Queen Bee explains.

"Well we...Urgh.....just have to keep searching for it. Let's go check on Madilyn." The voice says as they start to move to the door. The doors opens and out walks a tall slim man. He has dirty brown hair that is cut short. He has deep green eyes with specks of brown in them. He smiles at me with this crocked smile.

"Oh! Madilyn your awake! How are you feeling?" He questions.

"Fine. Well sore, but ok." I tell him.

"Ok. Let's do some test to see if you broke anything. I don't think you did because Tyson was able to get a blanket of Darkness on the the wall before you hit it. It helped a lot because I think if he didn't get it there in time you would have a shattered back because that was a strong force of light." He explains while being over a thing of water.

"What's that for. Don't you do x-rays?" I question.

"Oh honey. No. We don't have.....those..... those ex razes. We use our Elements to heal and to check if we are hurt or something like that." Says Queen Bee, who was standing quietly by the bed. The guy brings over the bucket of Water and makes me sit up and put my back to him.

"Now we are going to lift up your shirt and I am going to poor water on it. This is special water. It will project a screen and we will see what's going on in you." He explains to me. "Now hold still." I do as he tells me and the cool water starts to run down my back. I let out a sigh and the Queen laughs at me. But her laughter is quickly cut of by the doctors confusion noises.

"That's....weird...." he trails of. I turn to see but he keeps me in place and I'm stuck at looking at a pillow.

"As I keep pouring the water down your back the image gets clearer and clearer. And it seem there is something blocking what I want to look at. It isn't bone or any other body organs. It isn't even water. It looks silver and it's thick. It is also stuck to your body. I don't think I can get it out." He explains to me.

"That's strange." Says Queen Bee.

"Yes indeed it is. Well," he stops pouring the water down my back and I turn around to look at him. "You're just going to have to stay here until lunch. You should be good by then but just get some rest and I'll be back to check on you." With that he moves the water away and goes back to his office.

"Get some rest." The Queen says and walks out the double doors. I slowly lower myself into the bed think of what is in my body. I try to sleep but it seems impossible. I end up just staring at the roof.

.*.*.

"-with her!"

"Aaron! Quiet down. She could be asleep."

"Well I want to eat with her!!!!!"

I open my eyes to see Jayden, Aaron, and Winter coming through the door.

I must have fallen asleep.

"See. She is awake Winter!" Aaron says to Winter. He stands taller than her but he has this goofy more fun side to him, while Winter is more serious.

"Madi. How are you feeling. Does anything hurt. Good thing Tyson was there to stop you from hitting the wall to hard." She says.

"I'm good. The doctor says that something is covering the spot he has to look at. But I don't feel that much pain. Overall I feel amazing! And who's Tyson?" I ask.

"Oh. He is the guy that was in the room. He's kind of not that social. We try to avoid him because he gives off this evil feeling. But he stood up for you and that's really nice." Winter says sitting on my bed.

"Wait you said something was blocking the examination Olix was taking?" Jayden asks from the back.

"Who's Olix?" I ask.

"Olix? The physician?" Aaron asks. "He is what you call The dacter?" He says super confused.

"Doctor." I correct him.

"Olix is the guy that was doing your examination." Winter tells me.

"So somethings in you back?" Jayden asks really into what's in my back.

"Yeah. He said something was blocking the spot he needed to look at. He said it was silver and thick. It's also attached to my body, but it isn't organs or bones. He doesn't think he can get it out. So that's a problem." I tell him. They all seem lost in thought, even Aaron.

"It could be another element!" Aaron says excitedly.

"Wait. People can have more than one?" I ask surprised.

"Ya. It usually happens if your parents are two different elements. It is very common. But three or more isn't. If someone happens to possess all elements. They are known as Six. Which is the six elements. So ya. And it usually happens in one in every thousand years. And the only known living one is Aspen. No one knows where he is or his last name. He created the school. So the school is named after him. He even created Elementa. But quickly disappeared after that. We actually don't know if he is dead or not. If he was alive he would be 239." Winter explains to me.

"Wait. You don't die at around 80 or 90?!" I asks surprised.

"We do die around that age but since he is a Six. He is able to live longer because of the more elements in him. The more you have, the longer you live." Winter explains to me.

"Well that's different!" I joke.

"Yup!" Aaron says plopping down on my bed. "We are eating here. Whether you like it or not. And we brought you some too!" He says holding out something wrapped.

"No. She isn't allowed yet!" Olix orders as he walks out of his offices. "How's she feeling?" He asks in a enthusiastic voice.

"Good!" Aaron answers for me.

"I'm not looking for an answer from you!" Olix answers while smacking Aaron with a book. Aaron rubs his head playfully.

"Fine." I say.

"When we run your Element along the spot that is hurt or broken. It heals faster than normal. So you should be good to go for the day!" He says.

"Great come on! We need to show you where you are going!" Aaron says trying to pull me to my feet.

"Just take it slow. And Winter will be taking her. You need to get to class young man!" Olix jokes.

"Fiiiiiiiiine!" Aaron whines. Winter starts to walk me to the door with Aaron not far behind. I notice that Jayden is staying behind.

Probably going to talk to him. I think.

"Just take it slow!" Olix shouts to us.

"We will! We are just going to bring her to her first class! Or I will!" Winter shouts back. And with that we leave the infirmary.

•*•*•

Winter has walked me up to the fourth floor and is now walking me down the main hallway. We turn right and then left. Then right again.

"How many hallways does this school have?" I ask as she turned me left.

"Eh. To much to count." She replies as we stop in front of a large dark oak wood door.

"Your fourth class is Elementless studies. With me! The only time we have one on one time with professors is when we do our Element practice. Otherwise we are with the same people we where with at the begging of the year. At the begging of the year, all the years are split into six groups among their Year with a teacher. They are like our homeroom teacher and then we travel with our class to all our classes except our one on one time for Element training. You and me are in the same group along with Tyson." Winter explains to me as we walk through the door. We walk into a classroom filled with human objects I recognize. They are displayed on shelves.

"Hello!" Says a voice from the corner. I turn to see a young lady sitting with reading glasses on. "Winter, isn't it lunch?" She asks.

"I'm bringing Madilyn to her class. And it's with you, Cenia." Winter says to Cenia.

"Oh yes! Welcome to Elementless studies. I love learning about the people that don't have Elements. And I love teaching it too! And you are from the Elementless world right?" She asks me.

"Yes." I tell her.

"Good, Good. You can help me for pronunciation because us Elementals, suck at it!" She laughs.

"Ok." I say.

"Please find a seat. The bell should be buzzing soon. It is almost time for hour 4." And with that, right on queue, the bell rings. Winter pulls me to the front of the class, that I'm not comfortable with but go with it. We wait for awhile and soon students start to file in. I notice Tyson walking in and catch his eyes. He gives me a tiny smile and sits at the back.

"Welcome, class!" Cenia says enthusiastically. "You have a new student in your class. She actually comes from the Elementless world. Isn't that exiting!" I here a few groans from the back and so does Cenia. But she just moves on.

"Today, she'll help us with pronunciation! Come up here Madilyn. And what's you last name?" She asks.

"Evans." I say quietly while moving to the front of the class.

"Ok. Ms. Evans. How do you say this?" She asks me while holding up a very old looking wallet.

"Wallet." I say. I can even see money sticking out of the old, cracked leather. "Wait. Is that money?" I ask reaching for the wallet.

"Ah! Hold on. No one touches the Elementless object because we don't know what diseases it can carry!" She tells me while moving the wallet out of my reach. The boys in the class start to snicker. Except one. I notice Tyson just watching me. I quickly avert my eyes to Cenia's wallet.

"So class. Say wa-llet." She says. Everyone says it exactly like I said it. We keep doing this for the whole time, while learning what they are. I notice how bored I am and when I am done saying it my eyes just wander all over the room.

"Miss. Evan? Can you here me?" Cenia's voice says.

"Ah! Sorry yes." I jump. I look at the class and notice all the people trying to hold in there laughs. I feel my face heating up quickly and can't wait for the bell to buzz. Once we are done with what feels like our hundredth object the bell buzzes. Everyone scrambles from their desks and rushes out of the room. Winter grabs my hand and leads me out the room before Cenia can call for us.

"I love going here, but I can't stand Cenia's class. She makes it so boring. I even noticed you zoning out. Because she had to call on you to get your attention." Winter tells me as we walk down into he hallway and passing other Year 4's. They all look at me with disgusted faces and I quickly avert my eyes.

"The reason they are looking at you is because we never have anyone come from the Elementless world. If anyone goes to the Elementless world you are punished. It's not allowed. And no one has come from it like you. But you are the first one." She explains to me as we make our way down another hallway.

"Your next class is Combat training. It's not with elements. Instead it's with the normal weapons. Sword, crossbows, bows and arrow and so on. Then after that, for Hour 6, on all the floors is a big room where students go and study or do homework for an hour. Some just fool around but it can be helpful. And you aren't mixed with other Years." Winter explains to me. "And then after that we can go home but if you need extra help in a class you stay for another hour and work on that. And then you can go home."

"Wow. Ok. Do I do Combat Training in my uniform?" I ask.

She laughs. "No! Of course not. In our lockers we have our training uniform. Wait you don't have you locker yet." She realizes. "I have an extra you can borrow mine until we are done. And on Monday, Wednesday and Friday. It's the exact same schedule and then on Tuesday and Thursday, it is Element training with the whole school instead of Combat training with just your Year. And we practice with our elements. It's quit fun because you compete with the older Years!"

"Great." I say sarcastically. "I hated gym when I was in the human world." I explain to her.

"Oh, well you'll love this. You get to use your element!" She says with jazz hands. We walk down another hallway and Winter stops in front of a locker. It is navy blue with a white lock on it.

"This is my locker. We have different coloured lockers for the years and then for our lock it's our colour of our element. So mine is white because I am a Wind. You'll have blue because you are a Water." She explains as she turns her lock. It opens and she has decorated it with all things wind related. She has lights lighting up her locker. She has three shelves filled with books and all her school things. She then has her combat training things on the top shelf with other things. Under everything is open space where she has her book bag and outdoor shoes and coat.

"Wow." I say as she hands me her extra combat training uniform. It is black shorts with a navy blue top and our crest over our heart.

"Let's go. We have to go down to the main level washrooms because they are the only ones with change rooms." Winter says as she closes her lock. We walk down the hallway in to the main hallway and passing the stone, strong fox perched on the fake rock. We then continue down stairs.

.*.*.

As we pass the water fountain in the middle of the main floor we hear a commotion going on near the east wing.

"Just ignore it. The older years always get into trouble and fight. It's common." Winter says to me as she drags me toward the back of the room. We enter through a door and are met by the girls from our class getting ready for Combat training. They all look at who is coming in and Winter quickly averts gets eyes as do I.

"Oh and we have it with the whole Year. But we are split up into our classes and work with them for the whole year. Now I hate changing in front of everyone so let's go to the bathroom." She whispers to me as she pulls me to the bathroom stalls.

We quickly change and she bring me back to the locker room and throws her thing and mine in a locker.

"You seem urgent for combat training." I joke with her.

"No. I just hate it in here. I wanna get out as fast as I can. So let's go." She slams the door and the girls still getting ready look at us weirdly. Winter drags me and dashed out of the room onto the field.

Eleven

We run out onto the field where it is a sea of navy blue and black. I see people already forming groups and Winter pulls me over to a small group. I see Tyson already there trying to hide behind his bangs.

"Our homeroom teacher teaches us our Combat training and our Element training." Winter whispers in my ear. I notice that the

79

Dawn person Jayden and I bumped into walks over to a large group of girls all giggling and laughing. And in the middle is non other than Hazel. Her blonde hair in a tight ponytail that is hurting my head. I feel my anger start to bumble up but slowly I try to disintegrate it. It still remains but not much.

"Ok everyone! Run one warm up lap and then get swords and wait for me to instruct you next!" A man yells. He has greyish hair and greyish eyes. He is wearing a grey and black robe that goes down to his calves.

"That's Tejin. He's a Wind and is our homeroom teacher. I'll go introduce you to him." Winter says dragging me over to him as our groups starts a lap around the huge field.

"Tejin. This is Madilyn Evans and she is your new student." Winter says to him. She seem very comfortable talking to him like that. He turns around and looks at me. His eyes are wide open then become slits.

"Evans? The girl from the Elementless world?" He questions.

"Yes, Tejin." Winter says.

"Ok. Well get along with your run or we are going to start with out you two!" He orders. Winter starts running and I soon follow. Winter's hair is in a low ponytail and her white hair swishes along her back. We are running past the forest when I feel a couple of chill.

"You....ok?" Winter asks, out of breath.

"Yeah." I reply out of breath too. But soon I am seeing a figure in a different room. My room. Not the castle one, my Elementless one. I shake my head and I am back at staring at the forest and track. But then it comes back. The Shadow is in my room routing through my things. His long slender fingers grasping items and tosses things out of my dresser and then goes for more. He freezes and reaches for a picture of my mom and dad.

"You can't touch them!" I scream. He doesn't listen and smashes the photo and drops it to the ground. He wisps out of my room and I am kneeling, and looking at the grass. I look up and see Winter and people hovering over me. I feel my checks heating up with embarrassment.

"What where you screaming at!!" Tejin asks.

"I-I, nothing." I tell him.

"Then tell me why you collapsed and where trembling on the ground."

"I don't know." I respond.

"Finish up and come and collect a sword." He orders me as he walks down the field to a stand with multiple swords on them, his robe swishing back and forth. I get up and push pass the people surrounding me. Winter follows and we continue together. It's quiet the rest of the run, which I am grateful for, until we get to the place where the swords are. She grabs one and hands it to me and grabs another one for herself. I give a small smile and she returns it. We walk over the Tejin and the rest of our class.

"Ok. Team up with someone that does not have the same element of you." Tejin tells us. Everyone starts parting up and I look around. Tyson it the only one left. He walks over to me.

"Wanna be partners?" He asks.

"What element are you?" I ask.

"Darkness." He replies. "And you're a Water."

"Ok. Now go to a open space and start practicing. Go until someone is on the ground under your sword. Don't stab anyone!!" He reminds us. Tyson walks over to an open space and gets into a stance. I walk over and copy him. He doesn't say anything until I am ready.

"Ready?" He asks.

"Ready." I reply not really ready because I have no idea what I am doing. He lunges forward and I jump back. He smirks as he lunges again and I jump back again.

"Get in there Evans!" I hear Tejin yell. I lunge towards Tyson, copying what he did, and he easily blocks my attack. I step back and lunge forward as he does the same. We hit our swords and it makes a loud clank sound. I keep lunging towards him and then I try something. I run away and turn back to face him. He's running toward me. I then run toward him again. I jump and make water appear on my sword and clang it on his. He is surprised and trips. He falls on his back and I put my sword to his chest. I hear gasps from around me and notice a small crowd has formed.

"Ahh. Get the sword off me!!!" Tyson yells. I quickly move my water sword away and notice a hole in his shirt where it was and a slight burn on his chest.

"Oh my god. How did water do that?" I worriedly ask.

"I don't know but you couldn't have just put water around your sword in a split second of attack. That takes practice and some how you put it on in a blink of an eye." Tejin says. I turn to look at him. He doesn't look pleased. "You learn that in Year 6 not 4."

"Sorry." I say quietly.

"Get back to work. Tyson go get that checked out and Evans, come with me." Tejin says walking over to the sword holder. I watch Tyson get up and he gives me a death glare and storms inside frustrated by his defeat. Something about how he pulls his bangs over his eyes is weird and I can't figure it out.

"Evans!" Tejin yells from the sword holder. I quickly follow.

"Yes?" I ask nervously.

"Where did you learn that?" He asks.

"I don't know. I've never done that. I just thought of doing it and it happened." I shyly tell him.

"You can't just have 'thought of doing it.' Like I said back there you learn that in Year 6. And why did it burn Tyson?" He asks.

"I don't know." I answer again with my head down looking at some interesting grass.

"Go get changed." He orders and storms back to the class. I look at Winter. She gives me a sympathetic smile as I move to the change room. I walk in and realize I don't know what locker Winter put our clothes in.

Guess I'm going to have to guess. I think to myself as I move to the area where she put our clothes. I start opening lockers and slamming them when I don't find our clothes. I was to busy I didn't realize the thing behind me. I realize to late when something grabs my waist tightly. I twist my head to look at a huge piece of metal.

"What the-" I was cut short when it squeezes.

"Argh." I cry out loud. I try to manoeuvre out of the grasp but can't. I then try to collect water and cool it down. I start forming it around the piece around my waist. I move my hands away and the water obeys. It moves the metal away from my waist enough for me to slip out. I let the water drop and stare at this massive piece in the middle of the girls change room. I shrug and continue looking for my clothes. I find them eventually and start to change looking back at the metal ever five seconds to make sure it's not attacking me.

.*.*.

Once I am out I go to the fountain and watch the water move. I dip my hand and feel the water run through my fingers and up my arm.

"Skipping class too?" I whirl around, startled by whoever came up behind me. Aaron smirks as water drips from my hand. I give him the best glare possible and fling the rest of the water at him.

"Hey! We don't want to make a scene if we don't want to be caught." He tells me.

"No I'm not skipping. I got dismissed earlier because I put water around my sword in training." I tell him.

"Wait. You mastered putting your element around a weapon to fight. Even I can't to that yet." He says.

"Why are you skipping class?" I ask.

"Oh well you see. Elementless studies suck." He tells me. "I don't know how anyone sits through that."

"Oh ya. That was pretty boring. I had to stand at the front and say the name. It's even more boring when you aren't learning anything." I tell him.

"Well you had a pretty eventful day today. Didn't you Evans?" He asks me.

"Did I?" I ask looking back at the water, watching it move.

"Well no duh. You got attacked by Art and sent to the Healing Centre and you mastered something that is very hard to do." He tell me.

And you don't even know the other things. I think to myself. Remembering the morning and the incident at Dean Huckles office.

"Hey I gotta show you something! Come with me!" He says grabbing my wrist and pulling me through the doors of the school. We come out and see a path leading to a dead end where Jayden and I came from to get here. But Aaron leads me down a different one past the school. We pass by giant trees with leaves swinging from the branches. There are also many flower bushes with different types of flowers I have never seen and they give of weird senses. We go to a giant hedge with a tree sticking out.

"This is Aspen Tree. Aspen created it when he found our world. This tree holds all the elements. Come inside." He says to me. He leads me though another path surrounded by hedges and we end up in the centre. The tree is tall and had elements hanging from it. There are benches around for people to sit. Aaron leads me to one and sits. He pats the seat next to him. I laugh and sit. We just sit in silence until we hear voices coming closer.

Aaron's eyes widen a bit. "We don't want to be caught outside at this time, so let's go this way." He whispers to me and points in the opposite direction. I follow him down a secret path. Before going any further, I stop and look at who is coming to the tree.

"I don't know how to get her to him, Art." A voice says.

"Well we just have to try and get her in a remote location so know one knows where and who did it. I think I have an idea." Art's voice says. I see Art round the corner followed by Hazel. They sit on a bench and continue their conversation.

"I was thinking maybe get her to go past the natural habitats and out there. It's ocean out there and extra land for the Earths to expand off of. But maybe there'll be a cave or something to lure her into." Art says. As soon as he finishes there is a crack. I turn around to see Aaron beckoning me to come to him. I take one last look at Hazel and Art who are frozen in place and follow Aaron.

"Why did you stay so long?" He asks once we are out and heading back to the front entrance.

"Art and Hazel where talking. They started talking about something weird and I don't know what." I tell him.

"Well forget about them. They suck. Let's sneak you back in without the sirens going off. Stay here and I'll turn them off, then I'll come back for you." He tells me. He goes inside and I wait until he comes back. While I wait I think about what they were saying.

"I don't know how to get her to him, Art."

What did Hazel mean by that. Soon Aaron comes out and pulls me inside.

Maybe I'll just forget about it.

Twelve

I was lying on my bed reading a random book I found on the bookshelf. *History of Elementa.* It's actually pretty interesting. I was reading about a part on Aspen. The Creator and Founder of Elementa.

So this place isn't that old? I question. *Huh.*

A slight knock on my door broke me out of my thinking.

"Come in." I tell them as I put the book back on the shelf.

"What are you reading?" Jayden asks.

"*History of Elementa.* Pretty interesting. Aspen seems like a cool dude." I tell him.

"Not that cool. He abandoned us after he created this place. He left never to be heard of again. He left us with nothing really. Just our Elements and a few forests." Jayden explains to me.

"Where even are we?" I ask.

"Elementa." He replies smoothly.

"No, I mean our location. Where are we?" I ask again.

"In the middle of the Pacific Ocean." He simply answers.

What the heck!!

"Wait. So you're saying we are we are littering floating on water." I breath out.

"Yes and no. Aspen has created some land for us and whenever we need to extend the Earths add land for us. Then the Wind, Sun, and Darkness work together to hide us from the eyes of Elementless." He explains to me as my jaw is almost on the floor.

"So I'm guessing Aspen is an Earth." I say.

"Yes and no, again. Remember he is a Six. He can control all six elements." He explains to me as my jaw is still resting on the floor.

"Now pick up your jaw and let's go see your parents." He tells me as he starts to exit the room. I follow him out into the hallway as I hear a scream.

"What's that?!" I ask alarmed. Before Jayden can answer me a small boy with white curly hair bouncing around, comes running at full speed at Jayden and I.

"Hey August." Jayden says.

"I am so sorry! Hey Autumn get back here!" I hear Winter say. She comes out of a room not far from my own. Her hair is down in beach waves and she has on a simple white dress. She is chasing a young girl the same size as August. The girl has curly white hair just like Winter. She has sparkly light grey eyes meaning she is a Wind probably.

"Winter, I never knew you lived in the castle." I say to her.

"Oh yeah. I do with these two goofballs." She tells me while laughing.

"Are they your siblings?" I ask her.

"Yes. This is Autumn." She points to the girl. "And that one is August. They are 6 and twins if you haven't noticed." She explains.

"Nice. Where are you parents?" I ask. She doesn't answer and looks down at Autumn.

"I-I'm sorry. I didn't mean to." I tell her.

"It's ok. My parents left me and my siblings when they where 1 years old. I was 8 and didn't understand anything that was going on. They left us here and we have been living here in the Living Quarters For Non-Royals Hallway since and haven't seen them. It sucks that August and Autumn don't know there parents. But I take care of them with the help of Queen Bee and the King." Winter explains to me as August comes back to her. He looks up at me with big light grey eyes. I notice Autumn has the same light grey eyes as August and not clear like Winter.

"Hi I'm August, and this is my twin Autumn!" August says energetically as Autumn tries to hide behind her brother.

"Hi. They are so cute Winter!" I tell her.

"Thanks. August is very protective over his sister because she is younger by 17 minutes. And she is more shy than him. He also talks for her." Winter tells me. "I wish she would use her voice. I love her voice and I try to get her to talk but August always does it. It gets annoying sometimes but I just have to deal."

"Well sorry to interrupt this amazing meeting, but Madilyn and I are going to get her things from the Elementless world." Jayden tells Winter.

"You've been to the Elementless world?" August says in awe. "No one is allowed to go there. Wow."

"You still aren't allowed to go." Winter says to him ruffling his hair.

"I will make Queen Bee take me to the Elementless world." He says with determination in his voice.

"Ok. You try that, but for now you are not going anywhere. Goodbye and I'll see you later." Winter says as she continues down the hallway in the opposite direction.

"They're cute." I say.

"Yeah. They suck looking after though." Jayden says.

"Hey Jayden. I don't want to see my da-Devan I mean. I don't want to see him because he isn't my true dad, right?"

"No he is not. When your mom left she took you and married him."

"Oh. Yeah. I just don't want to see him. It will be awkward and I don't want to explain everything to him. Is that ok?" I ask.

"Yes. Well make sure to get you and your mom somewhere he isn't." Jayden tells me as we start down the stairs.

"Thank you."

•*•*•

I land softly and quietly on my feet in a deserted alley.

Where are we? I wonder. Soon, out of nowhere I hear a thump beside me. I spin around ready to attack anyone but it's just Jayden landing on his bum.

"You can put the water down." He whispers to me as he notices my hands having a water ball ready to throw.

"Well next time be quiet." I harshly say throwing the water at the wall.

"Whatever." He says rolling his eyes. "Where are we?

"I have no idea." I say. I start to walk out of the alley and onto the street. I see houses all around us and soon realize where we are. "A block away from my house. Come on." I say to Jayden as I start to jog across the street.

"Hey! Wait up!" Jayden calls out to me as he runs to catch up to me. We run up the street and make a turn to where my house is.

"This is my street." I tell him and then I then feel a shiver. I freeze.

"What are you doing?" Jayden asks me.

"S-sorry I-I thought I felt something." I tell him as we continue to my smallish house. Once I reach there I notice only my mom's car in the driveway.

"We are in luck." I tell Jayden. "My dad isn't home." I start up the driveway to the front door when I hear his footsteps behind me. "Oh.....um.....I need to do this alone. Please?"

"Ok. I guess I should give you some space." Jayden says sitting on the steps. I turn and take a deep breath.

You got this Madi. I tell myself.

I walk up and before I knock on the door I pause. Instead of knocking I just open the door. It's silent in my house except a sizzle coming from the kitchen. Probably my mom cooking.

"Mom?" I call out. I wait for a second and instantly there is a reply.

"Madi?" My mom calls out. She walks out of the kitchen with a confused face. Her eyes land on me and her face breaks into a smile then instantly goes to a frown.

"Where have you been young lady. Your father and I have been worried sick for you." She says as she walks over and takes me in a hug.

"Mom, I know what you are." She instantly goes tense.

"W-what do you mean?" She asks. I notice the nervousness in her voice.

"Mom I know you're an Elemental. I know you took me here and you are a traitor." I break from the hug to look at her face. It has shock written all over it.

"Who told you?" She asks with anger etched into her voice. She has never gotten angry at me.

"A boy found me at school and took me there. I've already went for one day at Aspen Academy. I know about Queen Bee and her son Art. I know that Elementa exists on an island made from Earths, and that Winds, Lights, and Darks, have cast there elements around to cover us to the Elementless eye when they travel near us. Mom don't lie and just admit you are a Water." I say to her as she looks away pure anger on her face.

"You will never go back there. That world is wicked and that's why I brought you here!" She yells at me. My mom has never yelled at me. I step back by her voice.

"I also know that dad isn't my dad. You married him after you brought us here." I tell her.

"Stop talking and go to your room!" She yells at me.

I stand there shocked. "My room isn't here and neither is my home. It's in Elementa. And I'm going after I collect my things!" I yell back at her.

"You will not go to that wicked world. You will stay here in the normal world!"

"This isn't a normal world for me! I am an outcast here! But there I am normal! And I'm going back whether you like it or not!" I shout and as I say it, Jayden bursts into the house.

"Mrs. Waker, you have-" Jayden gets cut of as my mom shouts.

"I am not a Waker! Never ever again! I am an Evans!" I have never heard my mom raise her voice at anyone.

Why is she like this?

"Sorry Mrs. Evans. But you have to let her come back. And you should come back too." Jayden says to her.

"No!" My mom says sternly. "And that's final." She starts to walk away when she stops. "He's here."

"Who's here?" I ask. She stays silent as she looks up worriedly. I then feel a shiver.

Oh no.

"What are you guys talking about?" Jayden asks. But before he can say anything else, someone comes through the door. We all spin to see my dad coming through the door not noticing us.

"Hey Pop. Has anyone called about Madi? It's been a full day and she should be here by now. Why isn't she back yet?" He asks as he turns around to find me, my mom, and Jayden all ready to attack anyone. "Whoa. Okay that is not normal." He says.

"Sorry Dev." My mom says back to her normal voice, but with some anger still mixed into her tone.

"Oh!! Madi!!! Where have you been? Never run away like that again!" He tells me running over to hug me. I stand there awkwardly as he hugs me. "Who's this?" He asks finally noticing Jayden.

"I'm Jayden. Sorry but we are just talking to Madilyn's mom." Jayden politely lies.

"Ok. I'll be upstairs changing." My dad says casually walking up the stairs. We are all shocked for a second before we continue.

"Madi, you can't go there." My mom says quietly so my so called 'dad' doesn't hear.

"Why?" I ask.

"Because."

"Because isn't an answer." Using her term she has used on me multiple times before.

"Don't sass me young lady." My mom says.

"Mrs. Evans you have to let her go. Waters are dying and we could use all the help we can get." Jayden says.

"That's especially doesn't want me to send my daughter back there." My mom says.

"Smooth." I whisper. "Real smooth."

"Yeah, no. Come sit down for dinner, it's almost ready." She starts to walk away acting like nothing happened.

"Knock her out with water." Jayden whispers in my ear.

I spin to look at him. "I can't knock out my own mom with water." I whisper back.

"It'll be the only way to get outa here." He whispers back.

"Fine." I groan. I walk to the kitchen to see my mom setting chicken on our dinning table connected to the kitchen. She then starts moving to the kitchen to grab a pot.

"Come sit down." My mom says. "Is your friend staying for-" before she can finish the sentence I grab a ball of water from a glass to my right and chuck it at my mom, it stays in a ball and smacks her in the middle of her forehead with a loud smack. I quickly grab another from the jug in the middle of the table and throw it at her again. Before it touches her it stops in mid air.

"You think you can knock me out. I am way more skilled with water than you are." My mom says to me letting the water splash onto the floor. I grab another one and throw it at her. She easily stops it.

"You think you can beat me!" She laughs. Next thing I know she is throwing one at me. I grab it and shape it into a sword. I run at her with my water sword and swing. It doesn't cut her it just knocks her down. She hits her head on the side of the counter, I let the sword go into normal water and she slips on it hitting her head on the floor and knocking herself out. I stare at her thinking that I just knocked out my own mother

It's the only thing you had to do to go back. A voice tells me from the back of my mind. I walk out to the living room to find Jayden standing there.

"Come. We might bump into my dad or I mean Devan so I'm keeping water in my hand." I tell him. Sure enough as we reach the top, Devan has just come out of their room. I quickly throw the water at him before he can see us. It hits him in the head with a loud smack and he falls to the floor.

"Well he's really bad with things that hit him. Let's go get your stuff." Jayden says to me. I lead him down a short hallway to my room. We enter and I noticed my things are thrown around my room. A broken picture frame lay on my bed. I pick it up and notice it was the photo of my parents that the shadow picked up.

"What happened here?" Jayden asks.

"I don't know." I lie. "But let's get my things quick." I walk over to my extra backpack and start grabbing some clothes. I then go over to my bed and find my book. I throw it in my bag along with some photos of my family.

"I just remember I left my bag at school with my phone and other things in there." I tell Jayden.

"Well have to go and get it then." He says to me. "Are you done?"

"Yes almost." I say while grabbing some more books that I haven't read yet. "Let's go. I don't want to be here any longer." I tell him. We walk out of my room. I take one last look at the galaxy on my roof. I have had so many memories in this house and room, and now I'm going to never see it again.

"Let's go before they wake up." Jayden says to me as he starts down the stairs. I soon follow. Once we exit the house we start to make our way to the school in an awkward silence.

.*.*.

"Go drop of your things and then come up to the Queen's office." Jayden says to me as we stand outside my room. We easily broke into the school and grabbed my bag from my locker along with my other materials.

"Ok. What am I doing there?" I question.

"You are getting your mark." He says as he starts to leave.

"Will it hurt?" I blurt out. He stops and turns around. I am scared of any pain and I don't want to experience any.

"I don't know. You usually get it when you are a baby so no one really knows. Except you. You'll be the first one." He says with a smirk. Then he turns around and continues down the hallway to the staircase.

"You'll be the first one." I grumble under my breath. I step into my room, dropping my things and feel a presence. "Who's here?" I whisper.

"Madilyn, nice to see you again." Someone says from the corner. I turn my head to be facing Art who is propping himself up on my desk chair.

"What are you doing here?" I question him shyly.

"Eh, nothing really. I guess maybe coming to see you." He says.

"Yeah, totally not suspicious at all." I say sarcastically. "Now can you get out. I have to go to your mom after I'm done dropping of my items."

"Want me gone so soon?" He asks.

"Seriously just get out." I say annoyed.

"You won't push you future King away, would you?" He asks starting to get on my nerves.

"I don't care if you are a future King. Get out."

"Nope." He says popping the p, and sitting down on my couch. I roll my eyes and quickly splash water on him.

"Get out." I say sternly.

"No."

"Get out!" I scream.

"Fine. Don't be so pushy." He says. I just roll my eyes as he leaves.

"Boys." I say. I then remember my things by the door that I dropped. I start to organize putting my clothes in an empty dresser I found. I then put my phone on my desk seeing many messages from my mom for me to come back. I ignore her as she keeps texting me. After I put my books on an empty shelf along with my photos.

"Done. Now let's go." I say as a knock comes at the door. "Better not be Art or I will, and mark my words, I will kill him." I storm over to the door and throw it open. "You better-" I get cut off seeing Winter standing there with a shocked expression.

"Hey?" She questions.

"Sorry. Art was just in here and he wouldn't leave. I don't even know why he was in here." I tell here. "What to come in?" I ask.

"Sure. I was wondering if you want to see some of our habitats or just hang out somewhere to get to know each other?" She asks.

"Sure. I need to tour this place. But I haft to go get my mark on my arm first." I show her my bare arm as she shows me hers. She has three super small, dark grey lines that curl at the end to make up her small symbol.

"Ohh. How about after that, we can go to The Edge or Waten or Axy or Trabik....?" She rambles.

"I would love that!" I exclaim to her cutting her of from saying any more. I look her in her clear eyes and notice something under her left eye. "Winter what's that under your eye?"

"Oh. I don't know. I've had it since I can remember. But it's a wind symbol. My brother and sister have it in the same spot, it must be a family thing." She explains.

"Huh. It looks cool." I tell her.

"Thank. I guess I should let you go get your mark." She says starting to get up. "You kind of need it."

"Okay." I groan lying on my bed with my head off making Winter seem like she's on the roof. "I was trying to procrastinate as long as I can."

"Well you can't do that because the Queen will not like you then." She laughs.

"Fine." I groan louder.

"Just go." She laughs while leaving. I get up from my bed and slowly make my way to the door. I see her enter her room two doors down.

"Fine. I'll be going now." I yell to her.

"Sure you will." She laughs again. I grumble under my breath as I close my door and make my way up the stairs and to Queen Bee's office. Jayden is sitting against the wall outside her office.

"What took you so long?" He questions me as he gets up from the ground.

"Winter." I mumble.

"What?"

"Winter."

"Haha! What did she want? Babysitting?" He asks.

"No. She wanted to go show me around." I tell him. "Now let's get this over with."

"Ok. It's not usually done here. But she has made an exception." He says while pushing the door open. We are met by Olix, the guy from Aspen Academy. His brown hair is pushed back under a cap and only his green eyes are exposed on his face while his lower half of his face is covered by a mask. He is wearing his clothes from today and is holding something that looks like a stamp.

"Madilyn. Come sit right here. This won't take that long." He says to me. I feel frozen in my spot when I notice the stamp has sharp, tiny blades making a water symbol.

"Go on." Jayden says from beside me. I turn to look at his orange eyes. I glare at him and slowly make my way over to the seat Olix has out. I notice the Queen sitting very quietly outside in a balcony I didn't notice before. She seems to be reading a book and doesn't want to be disturbed. I turn back to Olix who has on a smile that I can see from under the mask.

"Do you really need that. I'm not contaminated with anything." I tell him as he chuckles.

"Us physicians are supposed to were one if we are putting a mark. I don't know why but our head physician says so." He explains to me. "Now, hold out your left forearms please." I shakily put out my arm and he grabs it. He puts some lotion on a spot near my wrist and rubs it in. He then grabs the stamp and placed it on my arm. I wince at the pain and close my eyes. I squeeze them so tight they start to go numb. I keep squeezing until he says done and I feel something being pulled out of my skin.

"See that didn't hurt." Jayden says and I give him a glare. He steps back with his hands in the air. I turn to look at my arm and on it is a small blue water drop with two tiny ones beside it.

"You are free to go. Just don't do anything reckless to hurt that spot. It's still fresh." Olix tells me. I get up to leave, trying to get away as soon as possible but the Queen comes in. Her dress flowing behind her as she walks.

"Madilyn, did you get marked?" She asks.

"Yup. All done." Olix says. "And she's free to go."

"Good, good. Now go along." She says while trying to rush us out of the room.

Jayden closes the door behind him and we hear muffled talking behind the door.

"I'm going to go see Winter." I say.

"I'm going to go see Aaron." He says back. We stand there awkwardly and soon I turn to go leave.

"Madilyn?" He asks. I turn around to see him just standing there twiddling his thumbs.

"Yes?"

"Be careful." He tells me suspiciously.

"Okay." I say dragging out the a.

Why would I need to be careful? I question.

With that I make my way down the stairs to Winter's room.

Thirteen

"Thanks for doing this." I say to Winter as we walk down a gravel path towards an entrance.

"Don't thank me. I needed to get away from my siblings for a little bit too." She laughs as the gravel crunches under our steps. We reach an entrance and Winter stops. The entrance is a huge stone arch with water falling on both sides into big ponds. Dark blue gates stand, separating us from the inside.

"Sorry but I can't go in because I'm not a Water." She says.

"Oh really?" I question turning my back to the beautiful arch. "Why not?"

"Well because Wasten is where Waters live. Mostly pure Waters. Winzon is where I can visit." She explains.

"Oh. Well I'm not going to go yet because I want to spend the time we have with you." I tell Winter. "I'll go with another Water."

"Aww. Thanks. You are so sweet. Let's go down past Wasten and the others." Winter says.

"Ok. Let's go." I say following her. We walk back down the gravel path. We then stop and Winter grabs my hand.

"Hold on to my hand." She instructs me. I feel the wind and light come over us and wisk us away.

"Hello again." A velvet voice says.

"Hello." I say. I have become aware of the Light and Wind talking to me whenever I travel places with them. We soon are placed gently side by side on some grass. Winter immediately turns to me.

"How the heck can you talk to the Wind?" She accuses me.

"I don't know. They always talk to me first." I tell her.

"Wait, they?" She asks obviously confused.

"Yeah....Wind and Light." I tell her. "You can't hear them?"

"Well I could hear only the Wind and you. That's not normal." She says with a hint of jealousy in her voice. I don't ask her about it and turn my eyes to the view in front of us.

"Woah." I say breathlessly. There is a field of grass leading to a small cliff that goes out to water. Winter seems to forget about her jealously moment and turns to look at it.

"I know. The Queen doesn't allow many people out hear because they can ask the Wind and Light to take them to the Elementless world, but she allows some. I am one of those people." Winter proudly says. "And she allowed me to show it to you."

"This is so cool. You can see the ocean from here." I state the obvious.

"Yes. Do you want to sit?" She asks.

"Sure." I say plopping myself on the soft green grass. I lay down with my black hair fanning out above my head. Winter sits down and lays down next to me. Her white dress fans out from her body and her white hair lays on the grass carefully like it doesn't want to hurt the grass.

"You hair and eyes are unique here." Winter says out of nowhere after a peaceful silence.

"How so?" I curiously ask looking at the shapes in the perfect clouds.

"Well from the time anyone can remember Darks and Waters haven't always gotten along. No one really knows why but it's just a quarrel that has been going on for a long time. But they have never interacted. Your eyes and hair are a resemblance of a secret relationship with a Water and a Dark." She says.

"That's interesting." I say sitting up on my elbows, looking out over the ocean.

"It is." Winter agrees doing the same as me.

"Have you noticed how Tyson pulls his bangs in front of his eyes?" I ask tearing my eyes away from the amazing ocean to look at her.

"Tyson? No I haven't. Why do you even care about him?" She asks with a hint of accusation in her voice. She turns her head slightly to meet my eyes.

"I never said I cared. I just was wondering." I say back at her. With that we are thrown into a uncomfortable silence. I turn back to looking at the water and watch the water overlap itself and notice the little droplets of water splashing onto the grass by the edge.

"You know no one has ever stuck up for me like that." Winter says from beside me.

"Huh?"

"When I came to give you your food to be nice and Queen Bee wanted me gone. You said that I should stay." Winter elaborates.

"It was nothing. I just don't like it when adults send kids away without thinking." I mumble.

"No one has ever really been my friend." She continues as if she didn't hear me. "Apparently to Hazel and Dawn I am 'to nerdy'." She says putting quotations around to nerdy.

"It's ok." I say scooting closer to her.

"I love books and learning but no one really understood me." She says.

"Well I love to learn and I love book too." I tell her.

"Yeah. That's why I consider you my very first friend. Even Jayden and Aaron didn't talk to me before." She explains.

"Well then we got to talk to them about that." I say.

"Yeah. I would like that but now I want to spend time with my friend." She says giving me a big smile. Her black glasses falling down her nose a little.

"Yeah. I would like that too." I say giving her a hug. She hugs back gratefully.

"Ok. So now that that is cleared let's play a game or something?" She suggests.

"Ok. What game." I agree.

She smiles evilly. "Truth or dare."

"Find." I groan. "You first, truth or dare?"

"Dare." She says after thinking. I have to think for a second because I wasn't prepared for her to say dare.

"Eat some grass." I say.

"Ok....but I don't know if the Earths will approve of that." She says hesitantly

"As long as we don't tell them." I laugh.

"Okay." She says still unsure, but she grabs a handful of grass instead. She then puts the handful into her mouth and chews. I laugh at her attempt when she spits them out.

"Ok. Your turn, truth or dare?" She asks trying to clean her mouth. I go threw the possible dares or truths she can do. I finally settle on truth.

"Who is more cute? Aaron or Art." She asks.

"Seriously!!" I whine.

"Yes! Now answer." She demands.

"Ok....well......ummm.......Art is just weird so Aaron I guess. Don't tell anyone!!" I say to her as she laughs. We keep asking each other questions finding out things about each other through a cruel game.

"Ok truth or dare." Winter asks again.

"Dare." I say after many truths.

"Go jump into the ocean." She tells me as I stare at her in shock.

"I-I can't. I-I'll get caught." I stutter as she laughs.

"You won't. It's only going to the Elementless world because we don't want to expose our connection with the elements." She says.

"Ok." I groan. I sluggishly pull myself up and walk over to the edge. It's not a far jump and there isn't any rocks peaking out of the water.

It's my element. What could go wrong? I ask myself. I turn around and see Winter smiling from our spot. She gives me a thumbs up but as I walk towards her, her smile drops and her thumbs up turn to a thumbs down. But I stop and turn back to the ocean and run. I run to the edge and jump.

I have never been this devilish, but I jump and the feeling of flying through the air is incredible. I don't even feel like I am falling until I come in contact with the cold water. I am submerged into the blue-green ocean. My back arches and my arms come out to the side. I am embracing the cool water against my skin. My eyes are closed and I am relaxed.

I then move out of my pose and try to swim up to the surface but it feels so far away. I feel like I'm not making any progress of getting to the top.

Come on!! I scream at myself starting to panic. I don't know where I am so I decide to open my eyes to see where the top is. I open them and look around at the murky water. It has a green hint to the blue water and I see, instead of rising to the top I am falling to the bottom. I open my mouth to scream but it doesn't help. I just loose more oxygen. I flail my body around trying to get to the top. I try to swim but nothing is working. I am loosing all my oxygen and I am freaking out. But then I see a figure in the distance. My eyes widen as I see it looming closer. I franticly push my way to the surface but something stops me from moving up. It only pushes me down.

Why can't I move? I question as my breath runs out. But soon it's back. *What the heck? I can breath under water?*

"We saw you trying to get air and you couldn't get any." A voice tells me.

Huh. I think.

"We saw him coming closer and you dying so we gave you air." The voice says again as I remember the Shadow coming closer in the water. I turn my head around and don't see a black thing.

Thank you? I think.

"No problem." The voice says. It must hear my thoughts.

I swim up to the surface and break through the still water. I cough up some water and look around. I am farther away than I would have thought.

"Umm.....excuse me? Hello? But maybe can you help me get up there?" I ask and the water quickly grabs me by the feet and brings me to the grass. "Thanks." I tell it as it drops down and splashes on the rest. I look around for Winter and that's when something goes over my face and I scream.

"Help!" I call out.

"No ones going to help you." A deep voice says and something hits me in the side of the head. I fall to the ground but keep screaming.

"Shut up!" A very familiar voice orders me. I shut up and take a sniff. The bag smells like rotten eggs and it makes me nauseas. I feel light headed and my eyelids shut and then everything goes black.

•*•*•

My body feels heavy as I try to sit up.

"Argh." I say as everything comes flooding back to me. I remember being dared by Winter to jump into the ocean and the whole incident. I look around and my eyes adjust to the darkness.

"Where am I?" I question. Once my eyes adjust I notice I am in a cell. The darkness feels thicker and heavier in here.

"Hello? Winter? Anyone?" I ask.

"Shut up!" Someone orders. I smirk and keep calling out.

"Ohhhh......anyone? Anyone? Anyone out there?" I half sign, half scream.

"Shut up or I will come in and slice your throat before he does." That shuts me up instantly. I sit in silence and stare at a wall.

I have to find Winter and get out of here.

Fourteen

I've been sitting in this cold, dark cell for what feels like hours. My hands are tied behind my back but I'm not tied to anything. The person who spoke to me hasn't spoken and I feel like they are gone, but I don't make any noise just in case they do slit my throat.

"She's in there." The same person says. I don't turn to see who it is because all I see is black and very faint outlines of things. I hear heavy footsteps coming closer to me.

"Look at me." Someone orders. His voice is full of darkness. I don't turn to look at anyone because I can't and I don't want to. My head feels heavy and it hurts to move it. I keep looking at the faint outline of a wall.

"Look at me!" They say again. I shake my head slightly which causes me to wince and try to move away. They grab me by the shoulders and jerk me to look at them. I cringe at my head. I see a faint outline of a body in front of me.

"That's better." They say. "Now, tell me where Christin is."

"Who?" I ask confused, my voice weird.

"Christin Waker. You know her!" They yell at me in my face.

Christin Waker? Who's that? I ask myself. I remember someone mentioning that name to me but can't picture who.

"I don't know who that is." I say to the ghost of a face.

"You know exactly who she is." They spit.

"No I don't!" I spit back at them. They stay silent then they shove me to the ground.

"Useless." They say as they move away from. I stay on the ground waiting for them to leave.

Who's Christin Waker? I ask my thoughts as my cell door slams shut.

"Psst." I stay laying on the ground with my hands tied behind my back.

"Psst." I hear. My head shoots up and looks around at the darkness to find the voice.

"Psst." It comes again. I move towards my right and bump into a wall.

"Hello?" I ask quietly,

"Madi?" The voice asks. I recognize the voice and picture a white headed girl.

"Winter?" I whisper excitedly through the thin stone wall.

"Yes it me." Winter says. "Where are we?"

"I have no idea, but someone came and asked me about Christin Waker. I have no idea who that is." I explain to her. She sucks in a breath and doesn't answer. "Winter?" I ask. The next thing I hear is screams coming from behind the wall.

"Sorry!! Please!!" I hear Winter beg.

"Winter!!" I scream.

"Shut up!" The same voice orders.

I disobey and keep screaming for Winter.

"Quiet!!" The voice orders. I quickly stop screaming and so does Winter. "So much better. Now tell me about Christin Waker."

"I...don't know.......anything!" Winter says in between sobs.

"One of you has to!" The voice says. I hear a thud and hear a door slam shut and Winters quiet sobs.

"I need information before killing them." The voice says as I hear footsteps fading away.

It feels like days being trapped in here. The same person comes in and asks me who Christin Waker is and then when I don't share anything they shove me to the ground and goes to Winter. He does the same but hurts her. Then after he leaves, Winter and I talk as quietly as possible until someone different comes in and gives us water and some mushy food.

"Open the doors!" The same voice orders. I get ready to be picked up and questioned. They pick me up and their grip tightens.

"Put me down!" I scream at him. He doesn't listen and carries me somewhere. I hear Winter call for me. He then drops me to my feet and my knees buckle.

"Stand up and follow!" They order. I stager to my feet and try to follow. I bump into a wall and fall to the hard floor. I push myself up again and try to focus my eyes. I can finally see clearer outlines of walls and people. I see someone walking away and follow them. I try to find any exits but we just keep walking. I start to hear heavy footsteps behind me and turn around to see two people walking behind me.

"In hear." The person deep voice says and pushes me into another cell. He comes in to and pick me up for our normal routine. But instead of pushing me to the ground after him questioning me, he grabs a shape from his pocket and slices my forearm. I try to hold back my tears but the scream comes. He cuts again in the same spot and I try to wiggle out of his grasp. Tears end up escaping my eyes and fall down my cheeks.

"Hold still!" He orders. I keep moving and he cuts right beside the bigger cut.

"AHHHH!!!" I scream at the top of my lungs as my vision gets blurry.

"It isn't here." The person says and drops me to the ground. He walks out and slams the door. I lay on the floor breathing heavy.

"Are you ok?" A quiet voice asks. I turn my head to look around for the voice.

"What?" My voice cracks.

"Are you ok?" The voice replies. The voice is higher pitched and more angel like than the deep voices I have been hearing.

"Yeah-no." I say turning my head the other way. I see a figure against a wall.

"You'll be ok." They assure me.

"Who are you?" I ask.

"My names Emerson. I'm an Earth. I'm a slave for him. I am kept in here to sleep and then during the day I do things for him. Who are you?" Emerson says.

That's cruel.

"My names Madilyn, umm.....can you see in here?" I ask.

"No. Only Darks can see in the dark really well." She replies. I start to think of her answer to my questions. "You're probably wondering how I can see.....well the Darks that work here use their darkness on my eyes to help me navigate the hallways and see."

"How long have you been a slave?" I ask out of curiosity.

"My whole life. I think I was born here and my mother died so I took over her job as soon as I could and I have no idea who my father is but I hope he is alive so maybe I can meet him one day." Emerson explains.

"You two shut up." A voice orders from outside the cell.

"You got it Rodger." Emerson says enthusiastically. I hear a deep chuckle from the Rodger person. My eyelids start to close when something is heard. The door opens and someone throws in a girl. I see a glimpse of white and know immediately it's Winter. She lays of the ground sobbing quietly and the door slams shut. I wait for a few seconds to speak.

"Winter." I say. Her head shoots up and looks around. "It's me Winter." I say.

"Madi?" She says.

"Who's this Madi person? Isn't her name Madilyn?" Emerson asks.

"Who's there?" Winter asks panicked.

"Her names Emerson. She's a slave." I say to Winter and Emerson explains everything.

"Shut up!" Rodger orders.

"Got it!" Emerson says. I hear her trying to get to the ground. I soon make out that she is attached to the wall with handcuffs. I then turn my head to see Winter on the ground already, with her hands behind her back, trying to sleep. I do the same and my eyes shut this time.

Fifteen

I jolt from my spot on the hard floor with a scream splitting my ears. I look around and see Winter being dragged from the cell. I quickly look over to Emerson's spot but she isn't there.

What's going on? I question. I look back at Winter being dragged from the cell. I try to stand up and walk over to her.

"Winter!!" I yell as I walk over to the door. Once I get there someone pushes me back down to the ground.

"Stay low." A familiar voice says into my ear. My eyes are wide with shock but I obey this familiar voice. Then Winter suddenly stops screaming.

What is going on? I question. I look around to see two bodies at the entrance. I stand up and slowly make my way over to them when someone pushes me to the ground again.

"Stay Down!" They order. I look up and see reddish-brown hair and instantly know who has come. I stay on the floor while they do what they are doing. Then someone comes and helps me to my feet. I feel very unsteady on my feet but I hold my ground.

"Can you walk?" The accented voice asks.

"Yes." I weakly reply. They don't respond and lead me quietly out
the cell. Once we get out I notice the Rodger person on the ground
unconscious. I don't ask any questions as Jayden leads me quietly
down a hallway. I don't know where Winter is or how Jayden is
seeing in the dark when he is a Fire. We turn a corner and he
suddenly stops. He flattens himself on a wall and I copy him.

"Who's there?" A voice asks. I don't say anything and neither does
Jayden. Someone's footsteps start down towards us and my heart
beat quickens. Once they are close enough Jayden ignites a ball of
fire and throws it at the person. It illuminates the hallway and it
travels to its destination. The ball of flames hit the person in the
face and they let out the most horrifying scream. Jayden pulls me
along the corridor leaving the person thrashing on the ground.
Instead of walking, Jayden starts to run. We turn down many
hallways and we soon reach a dead end.

"This is a dead end." I whisper to Jayden. I see him nod and move
forward. He stops suddenly by a slither of a voice.

"You are not going anywhere." Someone says from behind us. I
spin around and see a figure. They step towards us and Jayden
pulls me behind his back. My arms grazes his and I hiss with pain
from my cut. I hear a deep, deadly laugh from the person in front
of us.

"You aren't touching her." Jayden says to the person.

"Oh....sweet boy......she was mine to begin with." The person
evilly laughs out the sentence. Jayden doesn't wast any time and
attacks. He lunges for the person and conjures two handfuls of fire.
He swings for the person who just laughs and dodges his attacks.

"You will never get me!" The person says as Jayden misses terribly. I want to help but my feet are glued to the ground and I can't seem to move. Jayden keeps trying to hit the person and keeps missing. I then see the person pushing something on Jayden. Jayden stops in his tracks and falls the the ground.

"See!!!" The person cackles. Jayden is pushes down on his hands and knees. The thing that is pushing him down presses down on his back and his feet don't move from under him.

"Stop!" I yell as I watch the horrifying scene in front of me unfold. The person turns their head to me and I can see a hint of a smile from under the hood.

"Oh...Madilyn, I almost forgot you where here." They say, smiling evil. I run at them with water building up in my hands. Before I can throw it, they move a hand and something stops me.

Huh? I wonder. They keep pushing me back until my back is on the cold wall. He keeps pushing and I can feel my breath running out. I close my eyes tightly. Then suddenly I'm released and fall to the floor. My arm finds contact to the floor and I cringe at the pain of dirt coming into my wound. I then open my eyes to see the figure on the ground on top of uneven ground. The stone around them is cracked and split in many directions.

"Come on!" Someone says through the darkness. I soon see Aaron emerge from the darkness, running to the wall with Winter behind him. Winter grabs Jayden from the ground and we all turn to the blank wall.

"Wait!" A voice calls from behind us. We turn around and see Tyson come from the darkness.

"Hurry up, Tyson!" Jayden says to him as Tyson carefully passes the person on the floor. Once he is standing beside us Aaron moves the stone out of the way to reveal a dirt path in the earth. He beckons Winter in first and then me.

"Are you ok?" I whisper to Winter once everyone is in the tunnel and Aaron has put the stone back into place. It goes pitch black for a second but Jayden conjures a ball of fire in his left hand, which lights the tunnel up.

"I guess I'm fine. Maybe. That person cut me a few times on my arms." She says. "Are you ok? I could hear your shouts from my cell when you where taken away."

"Well my arm really hurts because he cut me and then cut right beside it. It stings." I say to her as I show her it.

"Ouch. You should clean that with water." She says. I grab some moister from the air and splash it on my wound. I squeeze my eyes in pain as I stop walking. Jayden, who was walking behind me, bumps into me, making me stumble a bit.

"You ok?" He asks as he helps me up.

"Yup. Totally not cringing in pain from a cut really deep. I'm fine." I say sarcastically.

"Ok! Then that solves my question!" Aaron says cheerfully behind me. I shoot him a glare and he shrugs.

"How did you find us?" I ask as we continue walking down the dirt tunnel.

"Well....we uh.....noticed you two where missing and Queen Bee thought you went to the Elementless world. She was furious and sent some of her soldiers to go look for you guys, but I knew Winter will never do that so I got Aaron to help me try to find you. We searched the obvious places first and didn't find you. We went all around Elementa but still couldn't find you. It has been three days now and I was getting worried and so was Aaron." Jayden explains

"And I never get worried!" Aaron interrupts him.

"Anyway..." Jayden says sending a death stare to Aaron who smiles back innocently. "Aaron had an idea that maybe you guys world be in the ground. I thought it was weird but Aaron insisted we go. He then later found a tunnel by communicating with the earth. We started going down it when we heard a noice and this guy showed up." He says pointing is thumb back. "He was following us and decided to make his presence known by scaring us. Aaron and I almost took him out but he said he could help. We let him come and we then came to some weird stone. Aaron removed it and all I could see was darkness. That's where Tyson came in handy. He gave us the ability to see in the dark. We snuck our way into it without anyone seeing us. Then we came to a cell where they where pulling out a girl. We thought it was one of you so we quickly took the guard out and she fell to the ground. I noticed that she had dark brown hair and emerald green eyes so we new she wasn't you. I asked her where you guys where and she gestured to the cell she came out of and then scurried away. We went in and found you two sleeping on the ground. Aaron instantly grabbed who was closest and that happened to be Winter. She screamed so loud we had to tell her to shut up but she wouldn't. I grabbed you after and we where thankful that you didn't make a fit like Winter. Tyson disappeared once we grabbed you guys. And that's pretty much it." He explains. I stare at the ground shocked that they did it just them three.

Wow! I think to myself surprised.

"What where you doing at The Edge?" Aaron asks. We start to explain everything as we continue walking down the tunnel. Once Winter and I are done explaining I notice how long the tunnel is.

"This tunnel is long." I tell them.

"Yeah. It took us a while to come all the way there but we still got you." Aaron says as we continue. I then hear something snap and freeze. Winter also freezes and I look at her. Her eyes are filled with fear and her face is covered in terror. Jayden turns around and looks at us with confusion on his face and Aaron turns around goofily and looks at us with a smile playing on his face. Tyson just bumps into me making me stumble a little bit again.

"Watcha guys doing?" Jayden asks, his eyebrows furrowed together.

"I-I uh....heard a s-snap." Winter stutters nervously. I shake my head in agreement.

"Ok. Let's keep moving until we turn the corner up ahead." Aaron tells us turning around and walking to the corner.

"Aaron." Tyson says. "You won't make it. He's here already." As Tyson says that, someone jumps on me. They push me to the ground harshly and my head hits the ground hard. Stars spot my vision as I try to get this thing off me. I swat at it but my hand never makes contact.

"Get off me!!" I scream but they don't listen. Instead they lean down to my ear. I wonder why no one is helping me.

"Tell me where Christin Waker is and I'll let you go." They say.

"I already told you! I don't know a Christin Waker!" I yell at them. They laugh and speak again but lower.

"Tell me or you'll be coming back."

"I know who she is!" Someone yells from behind us but I am to busy to put the face to the voice.

"I don't want to hear it from you. I want to hear it from her." The person says to whoever was talking. "So tell me Madilyn, where is she." They say. I try to wiggle out from under them but it doesn't work and only squeeze me tighter.

"Even if I new one, I wouldn't tell you!" I scream. The person laughs a deep cackle and pulls out an object. I can see the shape of a knife and instead of doing what I thought they where going to do, they throw it to the side. I strain my neck to look at where the knife went and see it travel into a ball of fire cutting the fire. But before all light left, I can see the knife lands in its spot. Right in Jayden's left palm. I see his eyes widen for a second and then darkness.

Sixteen

Jayden's scream ricochets off the dirt walls through the darkness. So loud it could crack the earth. I hear a low laugh coming from the person on top of me. I am angry for what he has done.

"Get off of me!!" I scream.

"Only if you tell me where she is." They say. The darkness it easier to handle and I'm starting to see other colours instead of black.

"I don't know who and where she is!" I shout at them. I see them shake their head and lean forward. I take it as my chance to grab water from the earths soil and form the water into ice. I throw it the small distance between us and it hits the hooded face. The ice brakes into tiny shards, flying everywhere. I hear a small scream coming from him and use it as my advantage. I swing my arms around the persons neck and yank to the side. They get caught of gaurd and land on the dirty ground with a hard thud. I swing my legs so I'm on top of them.

"You think you'll win against me?" The person asks. I don't have to see the face that he has a smirk plastered on his evil face. Next thing that happens is the dirt comes up around the person face. It covers his face and starts to drag him under. I hear a muffled shout for help.

"Madilyn! Move!" Aaron says from behind me. I jump of the half submerged person. My eyes are wide as only there feet remain. Then nothing. I stand there shocked at what just happened.

"Madilyn?" A voice says. I turn to see Tyson almost out of a black shield. "He's a Dark. And these are darkness shields that only Darks that placed it can remove. But somehow I'm able to maneuver it a little to get out." Tyson explains as he jumps to the floor. "Hey Jayden are you able to cast a ball of fire?"

"Well not with the hand that has a knife sticking out of it!" Jayden shouts, slightly angry.

"Sorry." Tyson says. "Maybe with your other hand?" He suggests.

Jayden nods his head and casts a ball of fire out of his right hand.
It's not as bright as his left hand.

"Sorry. My right hands is my weak hand." He explains to us. I
notice Winter and Aaron are plaster to the other wall by black
shields. Tyson gets to work trying to get Jayden out of his shield.
He moves his hands up and down and side to side.

"Madi? Can you help us over here?" Winter says. I walk a few
steps to be in front of them.

"I'm sorry." I say quietly as I try doing anything that might get
these dark shields off of them.

"For what?" She asks.

I look up at her clear eyes and sigh. "For making us go to The
Edge." I say.

"We didn't know anything was going to happen." She says. "And
also I should be sorry for not telling him about....her." She
whispers her. I'm confused for a second until I realize who she
means by 'her'. I nod silently. I finally am able to get Winter out
her shield after pulling it away with all my strength. She gives me
a weird look but decides against saying anything. I then move to
Aaron as Winter goes to talk to Tyson and Jayden. I look at Aaron
and see his face stripped of goofiness.

"Are you ok?" I ask, concerned. He mumbles a yeah and doesn't
say anything else. I look into his hazel-green eyes and notice how
pale they look. His eyes have the fear balled up in a tight knot. I
look away to scared to look up at his eyes again. I finally finish
and he drops to the ground. I walk over to the other group and grab
Winter.

"Can you look after him and maybe....talk to him?" I ask her, jerking my head to a shaking Aaron. She nods and walks over to him. I continue over to Jayden and Tyson who are talking in hushed voices.

"Need help?" I ask, cutting off their conversation. Tyson nods and let's me take over.

"How are you doing?" Jayden asks.

"Mhm?"

"How are you doing." He repeats. I look up at him and notice concern on his face.

"I should be asking you that question." I say. He laughs a forced laugh and doesn't speak. I'm almost done when he whispers in my ear.

"I have to tell you something." He whispers. I snap my head up from my work and look into his blazing orange eyes. "Not now." He adds. I nod my head agreeing and pull the last pit of dark shield of the wall. He jumps to the ground still with the knife embedded in his hand and a weak fire in his other. I notice that my cut isn't bothering me anymore.

"Let's get out of here." Winter suggests and we all agree. We then continue down the hallway. I keep looking back to see if the person submerged into the earth will pop back up and attack us again.

.*.*.

Once we are out of the tunnel, the first thing I notice is how dark it is.

"Is it night?" I ask. They nod their heads in unison which gives me a hint of déjà vu of Hazel and her minions rolling their eyes.

"Can we hurry up. My hand is throbbing with pain." Jayden whines as we head in the direction of Elementa. He drops his ball of fire because we have enough light from the stars.

We have come out of hidden hole on the grass area of The Edge. Aaron, who hasn't spoken a word the rest of the way, seals the hole up with more grass. It's like it was never there.

"Let's take the Wind and Light. It'll be faster." Winter says. We agree and all join hands. Jayden obviously at the end.

"Wait." I say. They all look at me. "We don't have any light."

"The stars provide enough to help us travel at night." Winter says as I feel the wind wash over me. Soon the light from the stars follow and we are all in the air.

"Where to?" The velvet voice asks.

"Healing Centre 4, Trabik." Winters voice says.

"Why Trabik?" I ask curiously.

"Because Jayden lives there." Her voice replies instantly. We are soon placed on the ground in front of a white square building.

"Let's go!" Jayden orders. We rush into the Healing Centre. People look up at us but we ignore them as we walk to a front desk.

"Name?" The reception lady says. She has dark blue hair at the top of her head, but it slowly comes to a white at the bottom. She looks up and her eyes are a startling teal.

"Jayden, Jayden MaZinn." Jayden responds instantly. She flips through some files and finally gets one out.

"What are you here for?" She asks. Instead of answering Jayden shows his hand and her eyes go wide for an instant and she grabs a phone. She talks into it and soon puts it back on the stand.

"Someone will be right out to collect you." She says. Jayden nods and goes to sit on an empty chair. We all stand awkwardly as we wait. People keep giving us glances but I just ignore them. I do analyze their hair and eyes. I notice that more Fires are here than any other element.

"What about you?" Jayden asks. All our heads snap to him and he points to my arm.

"Oh!" I exclaim. "I'm fine."

He shakes his head and says."You should get it checked."

"No, I said I'm fine." Before he can respond someone calls his name.

"Jayden MaZinn?" They call. The man is short with flaming red hair and startling blood red eyes. I hear some groans and moans from the other waiting patients as Jayden stands up and follows the person. We start to follow Jayden, but a doctor with dark grey eyes and amber-yellow hair stops us.

"Sorry. But only patients are allowed beyond this point. You may wait here or go home and wait for news in the morning." He says and follows behind Jayden. We all stand there silently until another doctor comes to us.

"Can you please sit down or leave?" He asks politely. He has black hair and pale yellow eyes. I read his name tag and it says, Physician Turnner.

"Yes. Of course." Winter says obediently and silently leaves. We all follow her until we are standing outside the Healing Centre.

"What do we do now?" Aaron asks from the back of our group.

"I have no idea." I respond staring at the ground.

"We can go back to the castle." Winter suggests after a silence. Aaron and I nod in agreement but Tyson stays silent and steps back. I look at him and tilt my head in confusion. He must see it and says something under his breath.

"What?" I ask him.

"I should go." He says uncomfortably. I look at Winter and Aaron for confirmation to allow him to stay because I know they aren't fond of Tyson.

"You don't have to go quite yet." I say.

"Well I actually do because my parents won't be happy if I'm late." He says looking down.

"Oh.....ok." I say. I'm never good in uncomfortable situation. I never know what to say. We stand for a little longer until Tyson turns and disappears into the night. I turn back to Aaron and Winter.

"Sorry." I say. They both give me weird looks.

"What did you have to be sorry for?" Aaron asks. His face seems to be getting its life and goofiness back.

"Sorry." I say again. Aaron just shakes his head and Winter rolls her eyes. I give them a sheepish smile as we let the wind and starlight come over us and take us to the castle.

Seventeen

I wake up to an alarm going off.

What the heck? I think to myself. I soon realize it sounds like a fire alarm. With my eyes wide, I jump out of bed and throw my door open. No one is outside or roaming the hall. I zoom down the hallway to Winter's room and realize the alarm has faded.

Ok? What is going on? I question myself. I'm standing outside of Winter's room thinking of what is happening when a tap on my shoulder disturbs my thoughts. I spin around to see Jayden there.

What? Is all I can think. I then remember last night and all the events.

After we came to the castle we went Winter's room and talked. We talked for a long time until I fell asleep.

Then how did I end up in my bed? I question. I look down and see I am still in my clothes from being captured. I look up at Jayden who hasn't said anything while I'm sorting out my thoughts.

"Huh?" Is all I say. He gives me a smirk and then decides to speak.

"What are you doing here?" He asks.

"Well. I should be asking you that question." I say to him. "So....what are you doing here?"

He laughs a small laugh and answers. "I was released from the Healing Centre. They took out the knife and tried to fix my hand as much as they could. But it ended up being that no fire can come to my left hand anymore." He explains to me. "Now. Your turn, what are you doing here?"

I roll my eyes, but answer him. "I heard an alarm."

"What alarm?" He asks.

"I don't know. That's the problem. I was woken up and it sounded like a fire alarm. I went out in the hallway and no one else was up. I then came here and realized the alarm has faded. So I don't know!" I almost yell the last part.

"Calm down. Clam down. Don't you realize it could be your alarm to wake you up?" He asks. My eyes widen and I slip past him to my room. I hear him laughing from behind me.

How can that be funny? I ask myself. I shake my head in annoyance.

"Madi! Wait!" Jayden calls after me. I make it to my door and slam it shut. I then curl up in my bed and realize how tired I still am.

What time is it? I question and look over at the clock. I read 2:34am and I almost fall out of bed. My anger grows and I realize who did this. I stomp over to my door and throw it open. Jayden is still there with a confused expression on his face as I push past him.

"Where are you going?" He asks following me.

"Aaron." I flatly state. I feel my anger trying to burst from me and I know people can practically see smoke coming out of my ears

"Do you even know where he lives?" He asks. I don't even have to look at him to know he has a stupid smirk on his face.

"No. But you are coming with me to find him." I angrily state.

"Wow. Someone's angry. Only Fires get this angry." He tells me.

"I don't care if I am a Water or a Fire! Whatever! I'm finding Aaron and..." I stop and realize I don't know what I'll do once I find him. Jayden notices and smirks again.

"Will you stop smirking!" I yell at him. He shakes his head no. I roll my eyes at him as he speaks.

"Don't know what to do to him?" He asks my previous thoughts. I shake my head and he grabs my shoulders turning me around. "How about let's get you back to your room before you rip someone's ear off and I'll go....uh...find the Queen." He hesitates. I turn to look at him.

"Why did you hesitate there?" I accuse him.

"Nothing." He looks at me and swallows.

"I know somethings up. What are you hiding?" I ask, my eyes narrowing into slits.

"Nothing." He responds to quick. I shake my head and turn to go back to my room. "I'll see you tomorrow Jayden." I sigh and close my door. I slide against it to the floor and shut my eyes. Blackness slowly takes over me.

•*•*•

I'm in the tunnel again. Jayden is off to the side with a knife to his chest. Instead of alive and against the wall, he is dead against the wall. Winter and Aaron have met the same fate. Only Tyson and me remain.

"Tyson?" I ask. He is standing motionless in the middle of the tunnel and I'm facing him.

"Tyson?" I ask again. Instead of responding his eyes flicker to mine and instead of a water blue they are black bottomless pits. Even the white part is black. Then his black hair and face is covered my a hood. I step back scared because it isn't Tyson anymore. It's the other Dark guy.

"Madilyn." He says evilly to me. "Tell me where she is or Tyson gets it." And just like that, Tyson is in his arms with a knife pressed to his throat. His expression is emotionless. Unfazed.

"Don't-" I start but he cuts right through his neck. Tyson drops to the ground and he lays dead on the dirt. I want to scream but nothing comes out. Suddenly I can't move. I look down at my feet and they are covered in a black sludge. He comes closer to me with another knife. This time it has a clear blackness around it. My eyes widen at the sight and try to move, but the sludge holds firm. I try anything to get free and then I try manipulating it like Tyson was, I'm free. I turn to run in the opposite direction.

"Come back Madilyn! It's only one piece of information and I won't even hurt you!" He says from behind me. I take one glance over my shoulder and see he isn't moving. Then I hit something. I fall to the ground and he is over me. I let out a scream I was holding in. He leans down to my ear and I try to punch him, kick, anything, but nothing of my body moves. I'm not covered in anything but I can't move.

"Tell..me where....she......." he whispers in my ear, dragging out every word while his knife light drags across my cheek. "Is." He finishes and brings the knife down to my neck.

I scream.

.*.*.

And scream and scream. My head hurts from screaming and no one has come. The image of my first friends dead on the ground scares me to death. I lay in my dirty clothes, that I have been wearing for who knows how many days, my hands against my head, clutching my hair. My screams soon die down and I'm trembling on the floor. I don't care to look at the clock or turn on the light. All I do is is lie down, tremble, and clutch my head.

The instant I move my head, I regret it. A headache splits through my head and it causes more screams which cause more pain.

I scream for so long that, finally, I'm done with screaming and look out the window. Dawn has come through and beautiful colours shine through my window.

"Not everything is beautiful sky!" I shout at the sky, my voice raspy from all the yelling and screaming. Then the tears come. I sob onto my hard floor and tears stain my cheeks.

"Why did that nightmare have to come?" I question out loud through tears.

I cry for what feels like hours and hours until I hear my door open from behind me. I don't make any movement as a light comes on. It makes my headache split and I scream more. My screams sound like a crow dying.

"Shhh..." someone says as arms wrap around me. I don't care to see who it is as I squeeze my eyes shut.

"Turn the light down." Someone orders and it goes dark once again. My eyes unclench but stay closed. I don't want to look at anyone right now.

I just want to sleep without nightmares.

Eighteen

For the past hour, I had been laying in my mattress with my eyes open looking at the roof. Someone placed me in my mattress after they discovered me at the floor. I don't dare observe who it's far, I simply know they haven't left yet.

"Madi?" Winter's quiet voice comes from in the back of me. "Are you ok?"

"Winter, let's not push her." Aaron's voice says. I don't circulate anything. My head hurts like crazy and my throat is dry.

"Jayden is waiting within the library for us." She says as a hand touches my shoulder. I recoil and the hand is straight away gone.

"Maybe we ought to just permit her be and we are able to go to the library together. There turned into another intense out damage of the poison and many have already died." Aaron says to Winter. "We just where going to appearance it up and see if there are any ways we are able to inform Queen Bee that could forestall it. We simply wanted your help due to the fact you are the Water in our organization." He explains further. When I nevertheless do not say something I hear there footsteps fading to the door.

I bolt strait up and study them. "Wait! Don't move!" I yell at them which reasons my head to hurt and throat. I seize it tough and fall against my bed. "I'm scared to nod off." I mumble.

"What become that?" Winter asks. She comes over and kneels down to my degree. Her lovely white hair is in
french braids and she or he has on denims with a white blouse.

"Do you want to talk about it?" She asks. I shake my head sure and sit up straight. Aaron has a severe face on and is status in the back of Winter.

"First of." I begin and my voice is horse. "Aaron why did you try this?" I ask.

He shakes is head and answers. "I don't have any idea. I notion it might be humorous due to the fact we simply had a horrible experience and I just desired to make you snicker. But I failed to count on you to cry over it." He admits.

"That's certainly not the purpose I'm crying." I say. I then go on and give an explanation for the entirety that happened ultimate night with my nightmare.

"That's terrible." Winter says. I shake my head in settlement.

"I do not want to die." Aaron says from beside Winter with his hand over his heart.

"I bet I should easy myself up. And allow's cross meet Jayden inside the library. He might be looking ahead to us." I say. They nod and depart, leaving me alone in my room. I stay sitting on my bed for some time earlier than quick throwing away the clothes I became carrying and taking a short bathe; cleaning my reduce that hasn't gotten much attention. I put on a few black leggings and a wolf sweatshirt that I discovered inside the large closet, keeping my hair down and letting it dry to it's normal straightness. I changed into sooner or later finished and on the point of depart whilst a knock was on the door.

Oh no!!! Please do not let it be everybody dangerous!! I scream in my head. After hesitating for an excellent minute and standing in the center of my room having an issue in my head on what to do, I determined to head over to the door and open it. There stood Art and Hazel smiling at me.

"Uh.....Hi there?" I ask. If I did not realize they where cousins, they would be best for every other.

Hazel offers me her fakest, widest smile and speaks. "We heard what occurred. Is Jayden adequate?" She asks. I stare at her dumbfounded.

Why might you come back here to ask me about how Jayden is doing? What? Just move discover him!

"Uhm...He is doing k." I inform her. "He won't be able-"

"Oh, shut up! We just came to see how he's doing. Not the whole story. Anywho, in which he is!" She says to me as a memory involves the the front of my head. The memory of having the toxic bag over my head and me screaming for assist reasons a splitting headache and I take some steps again. I stumble a chunk and I don't experience strong on my toes.

"Uhm.....Are you able to guys....Go please?" I ask closing my eyes and taking deep breaths. I do not listen anything and nonetheless experience presences
. "I'm sorry, but I would like you to head." I tell them. I open my eyes and they're still there, staring at me with conceited expressions.

"Of path." Art says with a evil smirk plastered on his face. It takes each ounce in my body to no longer cross and smack it off. They flip and walk down the hallway hand in hand. I shake my head as I near my door and walk down the hallway, the identical manner that Hazel and Art went. They start to go up and I make the move to go down. Away from them.

I became attaining the fifth landing at the giant stairs when I recognise, I haven't any idea in which the library is. I stand like an idiot, searching around to see everyone with books in there hands.

"Do you want assist getting somewhere?" A voice asks beside me. A boy with dark blue hair with a touch bit of white at the pinnacle of his curls and flaming red eyes asks me. Against his olive pores and skin, he is sporting dark blue denims and black hoodie.

He ought to either be a Fire or a Water. I suppose to myself.

I nod at him. "Yes. I would like to go to the library." I say. He smiles a toothy smile.

"Follow me." He says and keeps up the steps. We go by way of my hallway and prevent just earlier than the Royal Hallway. "This is the Library." He explains as we keep down a quick hallway to a double darkish very welldoor. He pushes the door open and I set free a gasp.

"Do you like it?" He asks. I feel his flaming eyes on me but I don't budge or examine him. Instead I recognize the heaps of books and masses of cabinets, stacked to an incredibly high roof.

"Yes!" I manipulate to squeak out. I listen him chortle beside me.

"What's your name?" He asks.

"Uhm......Oh sorry! It's Madilyn Evans." I say, to distracted via the books.

"And what's yours?" I ask finally able to tear my eyes faraway from the sight of beauty.

"Xavier Rhéve." He says. I smile at him and say a polite thank you and Xavier turns to move backtrack the giant stairs. I then flip lower back to the books. I carefully stroll in and stroll down each isle.

This region is incredible!! I scream interior my head. I become to busy studying each title of the books and walking up and down every isle that I forgot what I got here right here for until I sense a light tap on my shoulder. I appearance at the back of me and Jayden is status there.

"Oh!!!" I say shocked. "Sorry!! I definitely forgot that I become meeting you men right here!! So sorry!" I say to him, setting the book I become retaining back on the self. He just smiles and leads me to the again of the library wherein a stone hearth is placed in opposition to a wooden wall with sofas and chairs scattered round in conjunction with a few tables. We walk in the direction of a analyzing Winter and a the wrong way up Aaron.

"Finally!" Aaron exclaims from his the wrong way up shape. "I thought you forgot approximately us!"

Winter looks up from her book and smiles. As she opens her mouth an elderly girl with honey coloured hair and light grey eyes looks at us with an irritated expression.

"If I even have to inform you to be quiet one more time, Aaron, then you'll ought to depart." She says sternly and disappears behind a bookshelf.

"I will gladly, Mrs. Libby." He says and falls to the ground with a tough thud.

"No." Winter says as she shakes her head violently, her french braids swinging back and forth. "We want your help to try and locate the supply of the poison so we will provide it to Queen Bee. She requested us in particular."

"Fine!" Aaron groans and sits down in his chair crossing his arms over his chest.

"Why?" I ask. Jayden appears at me noticing how my voice sounds.

"I don't know. She just did." Winter says and appears down at her book. "Let's get to work." Winter announces as Jayden and I sit down on one of the sofas surrounding the hearth.

Nineteen

"Winter!!!" Aaron whines. "Can we cross. I'm worn-out!!" He whines similarly.

We had been in the library for hours and Aaron wouldn't close up since the first hour. No one else lingered within the library. It became just us and a whining Aaron.

"No." Winter says sternly, like a mother speakme to her son about now not stealing cookies. "I need to find this supply so it does not have an effect on another element. You recognize what will appear when one element is long past. All the other elements go through." Winter explains.

"Urgh!!" Aaron groans greater.

Jayden rolls his eyes at Aaron's infantile behaviour and turns to me. "After this I sincerely have to tell you some thing." He whispers and I provide a tiny shake of my head.

"Now. I think it's miles beginning inside the lake set east of the gates of Wasten." Winter says. "It's an obvious supply. All Waters pass and touch it ordinary. Also the physicians have stated that the poison begins in there arms and makes its way to the coronary heart. It is likewise big enough to hold such powerful poison to kill many Waters-" she quickly gets cut off my Aaron.

"Blah.....Blah.....Water....Blah......Blah......Blah....Poison....Blah....Blah.....Lake. We get it!" Aaron says to Winter. She glares at him and earlier than she says something back, I speak.

"I apprehend. But will we realize how to prevent it?" I ask. They all take a look at me, confusion sincerely etched on their faces. Expect Aaron's.

"Well...." Winter starts offevolved but stops unexpectedly searching burdened. "I don't know. How can we prevent this? Or how does the Queen prevent it?" She asks. I nod my head in settlement.

"Well.....You might not be needing to return returned here because my dad and mom have it underneath manage." Says a voice from at the back of us. We flip to see a smirking blond haired boy.

"Art, If we want to assist, we will." Winter says from her chair.

"Well you might not be desiring to. Like I said. It is under control." He says with a grin and leaves us alone. Winter rolls her eyes at Art.

Jayden all of sudden receives up and I appearance to him. "Can I talk with you?" He asks me. I can see anxiousness in his eyes and it starts to get me apprehensive.

"Yeah...Of path." I say nervously. He nods his head on walks away to the library doors.

"What do you watched he wishes?" I ask Winter and Aaron shrugs his shoulders.

"I don't know." Winter says. I give them a glance and determine to observe Jayden out of the library. He looks at me nervously and I look returned worried.

Why am I frightened? I query myself.

"I would love to inform you someplace privately. I don't know how you would react to this however I don't want you to do anything damaging." He says. I nod and observe him down the hallway and the steps. We reach the hallway in which non-royals stay and he makes it to my room.

"Is it adequate if I let you know here?" He asks me twiddling together with his hands.

"Yes." I say and enter the room. I make my way to the sofa I even have in the room and he follows. He sits on the other aspect obviously looking to keep away from me.

"So...I don't know where to begin. But I uhm..." He tails of.

"It's good enough." I say. "Just spit it out." He appears at me with the most scared expression I actually have seen in my existence.

"I recognize who the individual is that attacked us." He says slowly. I examine him, tilting my head to suggest that I am harassed.

"Okay...." I say dragging out the a. "Is that it?"

He looks down at his shirt gambling with the hem of it. "I......Realize his call due to the fact I-I.......Used to paintings for him." He says and looks up at me, his orange eyes blanketed with worry? No. Fear? Then it hits me like a brick.

I stand up scared that he'll kidnap me too. "Y-you new!" I exclaim. He hangs his head down in shame.

"I'm so sorry. It become the best manner to break out my miserable home lifestyles." He says standing up. I step returned in reflex.

"W-hy?" I manipulate out of my all at once chapped lips.

"I became by using The Edge when he took me." He starts. "They dragged me down the equal tunnel, however in preference to placing me in a cell, he tied me to a chair and explained what he was doing. At the time I had just misplaced my little sister and my dad and mom acted like not anything befell. I was so indignant that I determined to sign up for them." He shall we out a breath and maintains.

"It wasn't that exiting as I was hoping due to the fact we weren't doing something. Then whilst you came alongside the man who I worked for all of sudden had a unusual interest in you and Christin Waker. He wouldn't inform anybody why. I then found out how desperately he desired you and Christin. So I tried to cease and guard you. He wouldn't let me and cut my proper hand. He failed to hit my fireplace useless however hit near hit. That's why my flame is weak."

That explains it. I assume to myself.

"I new about your kidnapping and informed you to be cautious. I need to have long past however I knew it changed into going to be bizarre. I lead Aaron directly to the underground pathway and pretended to recognize nothing. When we bumped into every different that night time I turned into going to speak to Hazel instead of Queen Bee."

"Wait why Hazel?" I ask interrupting him. I am still standing and he is sitting on my blue sofa.

"Well. She is likewise a part of this." He says. I am taken aback. "And I was going to tell her I stop this. She failed to apprehend and slapped me. She tried beating me up for leaving however I did not permit her. I didn't need to work for him anymore. I might as an alternative stay my terrible domestic life than a lifestyles of evil with Darks." He finishes.

I am bowled over.

Why?? Is all that is going thru my head.

"What's this men call?" I ask searching at him terrified.

"His name is The Dark. His institution is referred to as The Black Eyes and his fans are Darkens. He is also when you Madilyn. I desire I should assist you with that, however I know not anything of why he's. And he additionally is aware of I cease and might be after me too because I am an intruder and may spill secrets and techniques." He explains. I can't cope with this.

Why???

All I say to him is. "Go." I don't want to peer him. He nods his head and leaves my room quietly. I do not circulate. I am phased by means of this and can not address some thing. Tomorrow is my 2d day at Aspen Academy and I even have a darkish killer after me.

Great.

THE END